Skylarking

For
Thomas William, Thomas William
and
Poppy

Contents

Lenny and Vi

Lenny, short for Lenworth, was a dreamer. His father said he was under a cloud. His teacher said he could do better. His grandmother shook her head, clucked like a chicken, and said Lenny would come to no good. The only person who understood him was Vi, short for Violet, his sister.

Lenny was thirteen, Vi was eleven. Vi said she understood her brother very well. Lenny was stupid, and absent-minded, she said, but she loved him. That was okay with Lenny. For his part, he had a few things to say about Vi. She was a monster, he said, a little dragon. She was his cross to bear, but he loved her. And that was okay with Vi.

The youngsters lived with their grandmother in a house like a shoe-box across the gully from the supermarket. The house was surrounded by mango trees, an orange, a pawpaw, and some pepper bushes. Neighbours crowded round, dogs and chickens filled up the place, and Moses' goat searched for scraps in the street, and in everybody's yard.

The house had a flat roof, with just enough pitch for the rain to run off. One night, when there was no rain and the sky was clear, Lenny and Vi decided to sleep up there. But first, they had to get

Granny's permission.

'No way,' said Granny, 'definitely not.'

'Just once, please,' Lenny begged. 'It will be an adventure.'

'You'll roll off, or you'll walk in your sleep and tumble into the garden.'

'No, Granny, no,' he pleaded. 'Come on, be up to date.'

'You'll catch cold, or pneumonia, or rheumatism,' Granny said, 'stay in your bed. Roof is for rain, beds are for sleeping.'

It was like talking to a post. Lenny gave up.

'You ask her, Vi,' he said.

'Please, Granny,' Vi said sweetly, halo round her head.

Granny could never resist her. 'Just this once,' she said, 'and no skylarking.'

* * *

The stars over Kingston on a cloudless night hang low like lamps on chains. They do not twinkle, they burn, a million golden flames in a velvet vault. Lenny and Vi lay on their backs, a cushion under their heads, mouths open, staring at them. Lenny was receiving their spirit, Vi was trying to count them.

'I'm going there,' Lenny said.

'Where?' Vi asked. She had reached a hundred, and could rest for a while.

'To the stars,' Lenny announced, confidently.

'Granny won't like it.'

2

'Granny not coming.'

'Okay. How you going to get there?'

'Well, I going to wet myself with dew, and lie on the grass. When the sun come out, up I'll go.'

'That'll only get you as far as a cloud. When rain come you'll fall down, boof, right in the middle of Long Mountain Road.'

'I going to pick up speed, head for the horizon, take off like a water-skier, and just go on and on.'

'You'll hit Venezuela,' Vi said darkly, 'and it will hurt.'

'I'll find a way,' Lenny said.

'Never,' Vi said scornfully, and went back to counting.

'I will if I really want,' Lenny protested. 'I will if I really want.'

'Lenny,' his little sister said patiently, 'the nearest star is four light years away. So you mus' travel at the speed of light for four years to get there. You can't go that far, even in a rocket.'

'The Americans and the Russians them gone to the moon, and they does have rockets buzzing round the planet like bees.'

'That's nothing,' said the little expert on space. 'The planets are no big thing. Stars are far away.'

Lenny propped himself up on an elbow to look at her, the little know-it-all.

'How comes you know all this, Vi?'

'I asked Teacher. "Teacher," I said, "how far is the nearest star?" and she said, "Four light years.'''

3

'Teacher is ignorant,' Lenny declared. 'How come she know?'

'If you're going to talk foolishness,' Vi said, 'I'm going to sleep.'

She counted up to two hundred, rolled over, and curled up like a cat.

Lenny was left staring at the golden lamps, which swung lower and lower over his head. Drowsiness caught up with him, his breathing grew deeper, and his whole body relaxed. But his eyes stayed open until the splendid sky was ablaze in his head. Then, at last, his tired lids were lowered, and he fell asleep.

* * *

Needless to say, when Granny called for them in the morning, the children were gone. Their blankets, their pillows, and their shoes and socks were still there, but they were gone. Skylarking.

* * *

Granny was in a state. She went round the house calling for them, and round the yard, and out on the street.

'Lenny! Lenworth! Vi! Vi-o-let!'

People came up to her, asking, 'What has happened, Granny Williams, what's happened? Why are you crying?'

'The children are gone.'

Everybody joined in the search. They poked in the bushes, scouted up and down the gully, and enquired at the school, the shop, and the church. Nobody knew anything about the children.

The police came and took a statement.

'Open and shut case,' the constable said, putting his notebook in his pocket. 'The rascals have run away. Open and shut case. When they're hungry, they'll come back.'

A man from *The Gleaner* came, and next day there was a story in the newspaper.

'MISSING CHILDREN:
Riddle of the Shoes and Socks'.

A lady from the television came and interviewed Granny, standing on the roof. It was Granny's first time on television, so she put on her Sunday best, and looked very sad.

The Planet Knos

Meanwhile, Lenny and Vi were voyaging, past the moon and past the sun, and out into the wilderness of space. They travelled as they had slept, Lenny on his back, Vi curled up like a cat. They were awake, and they could see, and hear, and talk, but there was no sensation of movement. Looking up, down, and around they saw no sign of Granny's roof top, or Kingston, or Jamaica, or even the rolling ball of earth, spinning and revolving around the sun. They were two little dots afloat in the great emptiness between the stars.

'Where we are, Lenny?'

'Betwixt and between.'

'But we moving,' Vi said, as lights flashed past them in the blackness.

'I don't feel no movement.'

'Because of no air in space,' she said, flapping her hand as if she were swimming.

'Then how you know we moving?'

'Because the lights dem moving. You want me to explain about relativity?'

'No,' Lenny said.

The little girl was becoming a trial, knowing everything. It came from all that reading, and from paying attention to her lessons, things Lenny

6

couldn't be bothered with.

'Okay, Vi, if there is no air, how we breathing and talking?'

'Search me,' Vi said, stumped at last.

Lenny thought about it for a million miles or so, and then he said,

'I've got it. We mus' be suspended. We're in a state of spontaneous suspension.' It sounded good, even if it didn't mean anything, and Lenny was proud of it.

Vi didn't answer. She was looking at a great cartwheel of stars, a galaxy. She couldn't tell whether it was a thousand or a trillion miles across, but it was revolving slowly as it passed away, beyond their comprehension.

* * *

Bump.

* * *

Vi stretched and straightened. Lenny sat up.

'Well, dream done, finished,' she said, reaching for her shoes and socks. 'We can go downstairs for fruit and porridge.'

'No, Vi,' Lenny said, looking around, 'no porridge for you this morning.'

They were in the strangest place he'd ever seen. It was a fluffy, yellow desert, made of dust, stretching in all directions. In the distance, red clouds rose on the horizon like cliffs or mountain ranges. The sky was black.

7

'I don't like it here,' Vi said.

'Me nor,' Lenny replied, 'an' especially, I don't like being out in the middle. We can walk over to that rock yonder. We can climb on it, or shelter under it, or something.'

'Yes,' Vi said, 'and we can give it a name.'

So they stood up, barefoot in their pyjamas, and walked towards the rock. But the yellow dust was soft and dry, and would not bear their weight. They sank to their knees as they walked, and struggled, and sank deeper, to their hips, to their waists . . .

'Hold hands,' Lenny said. 'Hold on Vi!' he shouted, and took her hand. 'Hold on, Vi!'

They fell, right through the yellow dust. They fell, and fell, and bump. Bump again. Bump.

* * *

The new place was all blue and green, mossy and wet. They landed softly in a thicket of things like giant ferns, and struggling out of them reached a grey stone beside a tiny stream which sparkled silver in the gloom.

Lenny, on the stone, looked around him, taking stock. The blue-green surrounded him in swirling shapes he could not name, shapes like shadows, or like dreams. He could only recognize himself and little Vi, two children lost beside a silver stream.

'You breathing, Lenny?'

'Puffing and panting.'

'Better than nothing.'

'Yes. You break any bones?'

8

'No,' Vi said, testing her limbs in turn.

'I'm thirsty.'

They looked down at the stream.

'You think is water, Vi?' Lenny asked.

'Could be, may be, search me,' the genius replied. 'Hydrogen and oxygen are common in the universe.'

Lenny dipped his finger in the stream and held it to his nose.

'Could be poison.'

'Taste it.'

'You try.'

'No.'

'Okay,' Vi said, 'I will. I mean, we come I don't know how far, to somewhere, I don't know where, and we have no way of going back, dead or alive, so we might as well . . .'

They crouched by the stream, scooped up the liquid in their cupped hands, and drank. It was good. It tasted like coconut water. It tasted like home.

Lenny felt a warm glow come over him, a feeling that all was well, and was going to be well. He looked at Vi, who was smiling, and he knew she felt the same.

'If you can drink the water, it's an okay place,' he said. 'This is a friendly star.'

'Planet,' Vi corrected him, and they started arguing again.

'But you said planets were near, and stars were far away. This is far away.'

9

Vi shook her head and sighed, 'Lenny, why you so ignorant? Stars are suns, right? And suns have planets going round them, right? So this is a planet in a different star.'

Lenny decided it wasn't important. What was important was that he was getting hungry.

'Let's go find something to eat.'

They started out in the blue-green gloom, following the stream. Each step they took was giant, as if they were in some hop-step-and-jump competition, joyfully leaping from bank to bank. They came to a passage between cliffs, like a doorway to another world. Down below was a great plain.

The plain was chequered in the colours of crops, and divided into fields. It stretched towards a distant sea, or lake, chock full of islands, looking at a distance like floating lily-pads. Beyond that lay another plain, sloping gently upwards, larger than the first, and at the very limit of their vision something towered. Was it a mountain, or a cloud? It could be either, but it glowed and shimmered like a crystal city.

'Is where we're going!' Lenny said. 'That's it!'

'It what?'

'Where we're going.'

'Well, I don't want to go.' Vi sat down in the dust and began to cry. 'I want to go home. I want to go back to Jamaica, and to Granny.'

'Shame on you, Vi!' he said, 'this is a great adventure, we zillions of miles from Kingston, from daily trials and tribulations, from hot, from cold . . .'

'You mean we dead?' Vi interrupted.

'No, no,' he replied grandly, 'we just translated to the stars!'

Lenny was talking foolishness again, and Vi was not interested. She was looking at something over his shoulder.

'AAAAH!!' Vi screamed, jumping to her feet, and grabbing hold of him, 'AAAH!' She clung to Lenny, quivering like a bamboo.

'See dat?' she screamed, and pointed.

'See what? See what?' Lenny said, looking in the direction of her shaking finger.

'Dat!'

'What?'

'You don' see it?'

'No.'

'Aaah! Aaah! Aaah!' said Vi, excitedly, but each time more softly, 'it going, going, gone.'

'Violet,' Lenny said in a formal tone, sounding like a preacher or a doctor. 'Is what you see, my girl? Or is what you think you see?'

'A Thing,' she said dreamily, 'wid eyes. A thing like a great jelly-fish with eyes, just hanging there, over there, just there.'

'It minding its own business, or interested in us?'

'Looking at me, watching me. How come you never see it?'

'Well, maybe here in this place things appear to who they want, but not to everybody. Like duppies.

11

Some people see duppies, some don't.'

'That was no duppy,' Vi said. 'It was a spy, watching me.'

'Don't fret,' Lenny said. 'Come on, Vi, let's go.'

'Where?'

'Forward.'

The Prisoner in the Rock

So forward they went, down to the fields of red and blue, stretched out on a gently sloping plain. The fields were divided into rows, and each row contained some leathery-looking plants like cactus, bearing what could be fruit, pale yellow globes that glistened. Between the rows, a horde of tubby, metallic-looking creations moved. They were round, like vacuum cleaners, with long arms flickering, picking the fruit (if fruit it was), and passing it into open carts that followed them obediently like dogs.

When they were close enough, the children stopped, and looked down a row at all this activity. As fast as the fruit was picked, it grew again, and the little vacuum cleaner things worked desperately to keep up.

'Is people dem?'

'Which?' Vi said, 'The plants, the pickers, or the carts?'

'Let's wait and see.'

One was approaching, coming down the row towards them, its whirling arms denuding the cacti of their fruit. And like a juggler tossing it, never missing, into the cart that followed, never full.

When it was almost upon them, the picker

turned around and started up the row again, picking and loading, picking and loading into the distance.

'It's a machine,' Vi said.

'How you know?'

'Because it following a program and don't notice us. But it must have people somewhere, people smart enough to make a machine like that.'

'Right.'

Lenny went to the nearest of the cactus plants and picked one of the fruit.

'You want a taste?' he asked Vi.

'You first.'

Lenny bit into it. It was like an orange filled with honey, delicious. He gave one to Vi, and they sat down, munching happily.

Lenny encountered what he thought was a seed, and spat it out. When the seed hit the ground, it split, and out of it came a tiny lizard with too many legs. The lizard started to grow before his eyes.

'Ugh!' Lenny said. 'In a lizard beauty contest, that thing would come last.'

'What thing?'

'The lizard thing.'

'I don't see any lizard thing.'

The tables were turned. Now he was seeing things, and Vi wasn't. Meanwhile the lizard thing kept growing until it was about the size of a dog, and wagged its tail at him. Then it turned around, waving its extra legs at him, beckoning them to follow.

14

'It showing us where to go,' Lenny said.

'It what do what?' Vi asked, baffled.

Lenny rose, 'Just come along, Vi.'

The lizard led the way down to the shore of the lake, pointed at one of the islands with all its arms and legs, jumped into the water and swam away.

'Let's go,' Lenny said.

'Where?'

'To the island.'

* * *

The swimming was easy, as the walking had been. They tied their pyjamas around their heads so they wouldn't be weighed down, and struck out for the island. Lenny swam his famous freestyle, and Vi, more sedately, breaststroked her way across. Safe on dry land, they dressed again, and set out to explore.

The island was small, with a cover like blue plastic crab grass, and a pile of boulders in the middle, dark rocks with purple veins. There was no sign of their lizard guide.

'It mus' have gone under the rock,' Lenny said. 'Is lead it lead us here because dis place safe. I mean, here is water, and the rock for shelter, and ...' He leaned down to pick a blade of grass, and chewed it. It was sweet and minty. 'And if push come to shove,' Lenny went on, 'we can eat grass. We have time to take stock.'

'Take stock. Okay. What we know? This planet is smaller than earth.'

'Oh, yes?'

'Yes.'

'How you know?'

'Here is not so much gravity. We bounce when we walk, and swim like flying fish, and the only problem is the puffing and panting as if we were always climbing the Peak.'

'So, how you know is a small planet?'

'You weigh light, you know, Lenny,' Vi said impatiently, 'and all you weigh is the pull of the planet. The bigger the planet the stronger the pull, so if you bounce up and down you on a small planet.'

Lenny sniffed and pondered. Vi chewed some grass, pleased with herself.

'Okay, Vi, is where the sun? Answer me that! You said every star has a sun, right, and planets go round the sun. So, is where the sun?'

Vi was unperturbed. She looked up and down. She looked right and left. There was no sun to be seen, and the light was all the same, a pale yellow light, filtered through dust. The problem required brain power.

'This planet,' the genius said after a while, 'in my opinion, is like a coconut, with a husk outside and a shell inside. The place we land on first is like a husk, soft. The sky was black at the time, so it was night. Before day could break we tumbled t'ru the husk and landed on the shell. The sun still up there somewhere,' she concluded triumphantly, 'but we just can' see it.'

16

'And you go tell me the inside is filled with trillions of tons of coconut water,' Lenny sneered.

'Lenny, is no use talking to you. Your brain not scientific.'

'You wrong,' replied Lenny. 'My brain scientific enough to tell you that what we have here is a small planet with a hidden sun. It full of duppies, duppy jelly-fish, and duppy lizards . . .'

'What I want to know,' Vi said, 'is what the people like?'

Lenny didn't answer her. He seemed to have gone into some kind of a trance. He was sitting there, cross-legged, staring straight in front of him, seeing nothing.

'The people are wicked!' Lenny said. His voice had gone all cracked and gravelly, like a load of rockstone tumbling out the back of a truck. 'The people are wicked!' he croaked.

'Lenny!' Vi called, trying to wake him.

But the cracked voice kept coming out of Lenny.

'They call themselves Beings. They came from far away in space ships. They found a happy, simple planet. They captured us. They beat and tortured us. They made slaves of us, and worked our fathers to death. They took our homes, our planet, and our wives, and drove us underground. Then they sealed us up, captives for ever, and built their stinking city on our heads.'

Lenny paused for breath.

'Lenny,' Vi protested, 'Lenny, please, don' joke.'

'I am not Lenny,' Lenny croaked.

'Is who you are, then?'

'Parabolus, king of the captives.'

'And is where you are, Lenny?'

'Over here.'

'Here where?'

'In the rock.'

Lenny hadn't moved, and even Vi could tell it wasn't Lenny talking. This Parabolus person had got hold of Lenny's voice, even though he was inside the rock. Vi went over to have a look.

'If you run your finger round the purple veins, you will see me,' Lenny croaked.

Vi took a deep breath, and touched a purple vein. She followed it down a foot or two, followed another across, and back again, until she had drawn a square.

The square of rock glowed and shimmered. It changed colour and grew paler and paler until it had no colour left. It was all clear, like glass, and in that glass were the ghostly contours of a face. It was the face of a man-like Being, white as death, the flesh barely covering the bone, the hair stuck to his skull. The eyes were closed.

'Lenny, come look at this.'

Lenny shook himself, like somebody waking, and went to the rock to join Vi.

'That's Parabolus,' he said, in his normal voice. 'King of the captives. He said how there is a prophecy among his people. It say that two beautiful children from Jamaica would one day come and set them free. These children good-

18

hearted, kind, and helpful to others. Is dem would set the captives free.'

'You believe that, Lenny? You'll believe anything,' Vi said, and turned away.

The rock darkened, and Parabolus disappeared. Vi put some distance between her and the rock. Lenny followed.

'What else he tell you, Lenny?'

'Who?'

'Parabolus.'

'Who?'

Vi wanted to burst into tears. It was happening again, seeing things and hearing things one minute that were gone the next.

'Lenny,' she said patiently, 'how the children going to save Parabolus?'

'That's easy,' said Lenny, 'but it takes two. You stand on either side of the rock, touch it, and say the words.'

'What words?'

'What you mean, "What words"?'

Vi walked up and down for a while, and counted to ten.

'The words don' matter. De prophecy don' mean us. We not de right children, 'cause we not good-hearted. An' I don' like the looks of dat Parabolus, an' I don' t'ink we should mess with somebody else planet.'

'Is how you would look if it was you locked up for ten thousand years?'

'Mos' probably they had good reason to lock him up.'

'Anybody who would lock up somebody else, in a rock, for ten thousand years, mus' be the bad guy.

20

And the captive mus' be the good guy, right?'

'We should talk to somebody.'

'Somebody not here.'

'I vote against,' said Vi.

'I vote for.'

'Fifty-fifty.'

'Dat's it! Dat's de words! Fifty-fifty!'

'No.'

'Come on, Vi. We has to do it, 'cause we are in a prophecy! If you're in a prophecy, you can't turn round and say sorry, sorry I'm busy, sorry I can't help you.'

Vi sighed. 'Okay, Lenny, might as well.'

They took station on either side of the rock and put their hands on it. Vi looked over to Lenny. Lenny looked over to Vi, and nodded. Vi swallowed nervously. Lenny cleared his throat.

'FIFTY-FIFTY!' they said.

There was a crack like lightning, and a deafening, ear-splitting roar of thunder. The rock split open and a horde of spirits took off into the sky like bats bursting out of a cave, like a shoal of fish out of a coral reef, like earth from an explosion. They swirled, and swooped, and circled. Gathering force, they darkened the sky and disappeared.

Lenny and Vi fell down in shock, which passed into sleep. They lay for hours, in their pyjamas, by the broken rock, asleep on the blue grass. While they slept the light faded, without a sunset, into a deep gloom, and after hours more brightened again, without a sunrise.

21

The Crystal City

Lenny stirred. All around him there was a twittering, and a buzzing, and a chattering, trills, and squeaks, and grumbles. He opened his eyes to see a face looking down at him. It was a Being, at least a kind of being, though different from any being he had ever seen. The Being was tall, and black. He had large, luminous, slanted eyes, small pointed ears, and curling horns. A long slim face ended in a neat muzzle. The face was covered in short, fine hair, the face of a black antelope, with the horns of a mountain goat.

Lenny was frightened, but not for long. The expression in the Being's eyes was kind and understanding. Moving his head, Lenny could see that behind and around this Being there were many more. He and Vi were imprisoned in a cloud of strangers, all of whom regarded them with calm and curiosity.

The Beings had bodies like men, but all of them were slim and straight. Each had two arms, but only three fingers on each hand. Each had two legs, but he could not count the toes as the Beings wore soft plastic boots. Their clothes were plastic too, in soft and sober colours. Each had a belted overall, and a short waistcoat leaving bare their glossy arms and chest.

'Vi,' Lenny whispered, 'You awake?'

'Yes.'

'You see them?'

'Yes.'

'Good.'

When the children spoke, the twittering and the chattering ceased. Lenny guessed it must have been their language, and that the Beings had been quietly discussing them.

'You t'ink is help or trouble?' he said to Vi.

'*You* have brought trouble on *us*,' the Being said, 'but we have come to help you.'

There was something so kind-hearted about the way this Being spoke that Lenny grew quite bold. He dared to sit up, then to stand, and then to help Vi to her feet. They stood, but they were still dwarfed by the tall Beings, and still encircled.

'How come you speak Jamaican?' Lenny asked.

'The electrical impulses in your brain form patterns, which we receive, translate, and so deduce your alphabet, your grammar, and your words.'

'Is what him say, Vi?'

'It means they really smart, and if you think bad thoughts in front of them, you dead. So watch it.'

Lenny smiled at the Being. 'Okay, that's okay with us. We'll speak Jamaican, if that's okay with you.'

'No problem,' replied the Being, and all the others twittered and chattered among themselves.

23

'This mind-reading thing,' Vi asked, very seriously, 'is how Parabolus learned to speak with Lenny's voice?'

The mention of Parabolus brought such a look of madness on the Being's face that Vi regretted the question.

'Why did you do it?' the Being asked. 'Why did you free Parabolus?'

The ears of the whole assembly twitched forward for reply.

'I felt sorry for him.'

'How can you be sorry for an evil Being?'

'I can be sorry for anybody.'

'Didn't you think there was a reason he was locked up?'

'Yes, but, he said . . .'

'Come along!' the Being said, just like a policeman. 'You come along with me. Both of you.'

From behind his back, he produced a silver stick with a disc on the end, rather like a pogo-stick, on which he stood. A second Being approached with a similar device, and they each took one of Lenny's hands. Two more of the Beings did the same for Vi, holding her hands, supporting her, mounted on their sticks.

Whoosh. Whoosh.

Without benefit of engine, or of noise, the children found themselves flying, carried as captives through the shining air towards the crystal city.

* * *

The children were presented naked, because, on their entrance to the city, the Beings had objected to their pyjamas. They had removed them, and pushed Lenny and Vi into a long tunnel, down which they slid, into a room where they were washed by whirling feathers, like being licked clean by a million tongues and dried by breathing.

Expelled, they were taken through a maze of mirrors. These reflected everything, the children and the escorting Beings. As often as they changed direction, the reflections re-appeared, until they had no idea where they were or went, up, down, or right or left. At last they were catapulted into a vast room the size of two cathedrals, all red and gold, and into the presence of the Princess Oompallah, Ruler of All the Beings.

Oompallah was smaller than the males who had captured the children, but she made up for size with her beauty and her dignity. The body of a woman, the head of an antelope, the horns of goat, combined in a Being of authority and grace. When Lenny and Vi were brought before her, she was seated on a throne carved from a single piece of ruby-coloured stone. Above her head was an emblem like a jelly-fish with a hundred eyes, and her arms rested on a pair of sculptured heads with hideous faces like Parabolus.

The princess rose to her feet and approached the children. She was wearing a plain white robe which emphasized her blackness, with a golden belt, and one gleaming shoulder bare. In her hand

25

she held a mirror into which she glanced from time to time. It reflected her beauty, and she wanted to be reminded of it, which is only natural. The great hall was full of Beings, inhabitants of the city, who had come to see the two, small, alien creatures.

Oompallah examined their nakedness. She touched their heads, feeling for budding horns, and stroked their hairless skins. She sniffed at them, and made a disapproving face.

'Dress them,' she ordered, 'and not in those things they were wearing.'

Garments were brought for the children, like those worn by the Beings. Lenny got overalls of smooth plastic, and a waistcoat of a material like silk with bright zigzag patterns, and armlets suspiciously like gold. Vi was more simply dressed, in a long gown like Oompallah's, one shoulder bare, with a bright blue sash and silver sandals with a thong between her toes.

'Now,' Oompallah said, 'who are you, and what are you doing here?'

'I'm Lenny, and this is Vi,' the boy said.

'And we don't want to be here, we want to go home,' Vi said.

'We'll see about that. First, we have to decide on a punishment for you.'

'She sounds jus' like Granny,' Vi whispered to Lenny. 'She talking about punishment before the crime.'

'The crime! You freed Parabolus!' Oompallah

cried. 'You released him from the rock!'

All the Beings groaned and sighed, a sound like the retreating sea, for the thought of Parabolus' escape was too painful for them.

'Sorry,' Lenny said.

'Why did you do it?'

'We took pity on him.'

'You took pity on him! Well, at least you're kind-hearted. That counts in your favour.'

Lenny smiled proudly, believing everything would be all right, but Vi was still looking at Oompallah and saw no pity on her face.

'It was a prophecy,' Lenny added, by way of explanation, 'he said we were in a prophecy.'

'More like a curse,' Oompallah said bitterly. 'Parabolus told you,' she went on, 'that he and his kind had lived in harmony, happy on this planet until we Beings came, captured, enslaved, and tortured them, and imprisoned them in rocks.'

'Yes, that's right, more or less, that's what he said,' Lenny agreed.

'Parabolus was the conqueror, the oppressor, the torturer!'

'Oops,' Lenny said.

'Your mistake was to be stupid, to believe everything you hear,' Oompallah said, kindly. 'Parabolus is a liar, a cruel, wicked thief, a murderer of young and old!'

'Then maybe you're the stupid one, Princess Oompallah,' Vi said bravely, 'if he's that bad you should have cut off his head.'

27

The Beings sighed and twittered, like birds in a windy forest, as if they were saying 'If only, if only.'

'Parabolus is my brother,' Oompallah confessed, and her eyes filled with tears. 'Would you kill your own brother?'

Vi looked at Lenny, and thought about killing him. 'Well, yes I would, sometimes, but ... if push come to shove, the answer is no.'

'Push came to shove,' the princess echoed. 'I couldn't do it either, so I decided to lock him away, he and his kind, in order to protect the Beings.'

'I'm sorry,' Lenny said again. He was beginning to feel really badly about it.

It wasn't good enough for Oompallah.

'I want to make you truly sorry, and being truly sorry is not easy. You have to learn how to do it. You have to stop thinking about yourself. You have to feel you are only a grain of sand in a great desert, with no wants or wishes except to be a part of that great desert.'

'I knew she was like Granny,' Vi muttered rebelliously. 'I knew she'd start talking like a preacher.'

'You'll have to earn your forgiveness,' Oompallah said. 'First, you will be separated from each other ...'

Lenny was shocked. That was too much already. He was a trillion miles from anywhere, with creatures he didn't understand, and now he was to lose Vi as well. It was too cruel.

Vi found her voice first, 'Please, please. It's only

Lenny and me, only humans. We can't harm you.'

'You've harmed us already.'

'We didn't mean it. Please. I'm only a child. Come to that, I'm only a girl ...'

'Girls are just as important as boys,' Oompallah reminded her.

'I know that,' Vi said, 'but I'll be all alone. Please, please, please!'

'This is for your own good.'

'People only say that when they want to hurt you.'

'Truly for your own good,' Oompallah insisted. 'You have so much to learn. If you stay together you will form a gang of two, resisting us. If you are kept apart you will accept our teaching, and learn that we are right.'

The children looked round at the gathered Beings, their softly coloured robes, their curling horns, their glossy, fine-haired faces, and their large eyes, luminous and kind.

'So, to begin,' Oompallah said, 'Lenny will go out of the city to the edge of the great Unknown, and help to guard the Being World.'

'Yeah, man!' Lenny said. 'Great. I'll be a warrior! Brave like a lion.'

Oompallah gestured to one of the Beings, who came forward. It was the one who had captured the children and brought them to the city.

'This is your friend, Daroo. You must take care of him.'

'Me! Look after him! Yeah. Right.'

Oompallah turned to Vi, 'You will stay with me in the palace, and learn how to be good.'

'I was quite good before, you know,' Vi replied. 'I mean, I was top of my class in science, and Granny never had occasion to spank me like she had to spank Lenny ...'

She was interrupted by a voice from somewhere overhead, the gravel voice of Parabolus.

'Oompallah lies, she lies, she lies!' Parabolus cried.

All the Beings raised their eyes. There in the gloomy recesses underneath the roof, high above Oompallah's head, higher than the emblem with a hundred eyes, the ghostly face of Parabolus appeared and, disembodied, swung like a lamp on a chain.

'She lies! Oompallah lies! She means to punish you, to make you slaves, to beat you horribly when you are far away, too far away to hear each other scream.'

The Beings murmured lovingly and long, until their combined goodness drove Parabolus away, and he faded into the dark.

'You won't believe him anymore, will you Lenny?' the princess said.

'No way,' Lenny said, 'I promise, I promise to be good.'

Oompallah looked at Vi.

'Not me,' Vi muttered, 'I'm not promising anything. I mean to be seriously bad is one thing, but to be seriously good could be worse.'

The Boy with the Chicken Leg

Lenny and Daroo were flying towards the Unknown. Lenny had been given his own pogo stick, and Daroo had explained how it worked. There was an engine under the disc, about the size of a soup plate, powered by a battery the size of a coin, which had to be recharged every once in a while. The engine counteracted gravity, so the pogo stick had no weight, and then converted that power into motion, up or down, backward or forward, fast or slow.

'It's cheap, and non-polluting,' Daroo said proudly.

Above them was a yellow sky through which the light filtered.

'Is the sky always yellow?' Lenny asked.

'Yes. Once it was blue, but in the time of Parabolus, when the soil was all eroded and all the trees cut down, a layer of dust settled in the sky, and blocked the sun forever.'

'That's what we landed on. Does it cover the whole planet?'

'It covers all the Known.'

Behind them, as they flew, Lenny could see the

crystal city. It was not one vast palace, but thousands of adjacent and connected homes, built on the slope of a hill. Constructed of a substance like silica, or glass, it reflected all the light there was, making the city glow like a carpet of pearls.

Below, the fields stretched out, a careful patchwork of green, blue, and gold, watered by canals. Swooping, Lenny could see that the fields were worked by machines like the vacuum cleaner things he had first seen. But they were all different, doing different jobs on different crops.

'Machines?' Lenny asked Daroo.

'Yes.'

'They do all the work?'

'Yes.'

'But you have to fix them if they get smashed up?'

'No. There are machines to do that.'

'So what do you do?'

'We sing, and dance, we live and love, and think unselfish thoughts.'

'Right, right,' Lenny said.

The fields came to an end, and they flew over a range of mountains, barren and twisted, many-coloured rocks, pitted with craters, and eroded into jagged peaks.

'That's not friendly down there,' Lenny said.

'No, it isn't.'

'Anybody live down there?'

'Nobody.'

'Not so much as a tree?'

'No.'

Safely over the mountains, Lenny saw a blank wall of cosmic size rushing towards him. It looked like the curtain of a rainstorm out at sea, grey-black and laced with lightning, stretching as far as the eye could see from side to side, cutting the world in half.

'What's that?'

'The Edge of the Unknown.'

'I'm not going in there.'

'No, you're not.'

Short of the darkness, they dropped down to a little settlement of Beings, to the last outpost of their world. It was a long, low shelter, built of the same material as the city, a glowing igloo of goodwill. The shelter was home to some dozen Beings, stationed there to watch, and to warn the city of any disturbances in the great Unknown.

Two or three were gazing through the windows at the darkness half a mile away. Some were asleep. The others made Lenny welcome, just as if he were one of them. Listening to him talking to Daroo they learned the language instantly. They crowded round, with slim, grave faces, and with friendly eyes, with twitching ears and regal horns. They offered him a meal.

Lenny realized he was starving. Nothing had passed his lips since the first day, and that was who knows how long ago. He had no way of measuring how long the light was, or how long the gloom. Food in the shelter was spread out on a long table, always there, always available. Anything eaten was immediately replaced by a machine hovering overhead. Daroo showed him what there was, and encouraged him. The first dish handed to him was a bowl of fruit, the same pale yellow fruit he had first tasted.

'Lizards. It has lizards in it,' he said to Daroo.

'No.'

'I saw lizards.'

Daroo bit into one. It was firm and juicy, without seeds or stones. 'No lizards.'

'You have anything else?' Lenny asked, not trusting it. He was sure that whatever he chose would contain a lizard. 'What else do you have?'

There were many dishes, fruits of other sizes, other colours, bowls of leaves and flowers, beans and roots and spices, a profusion of appetizing-looking things, all foreign.

'You have any meat?'

'Meat. You mean the flesh of animals?' Daroo asked.

'Right. Or even fish?'

'The animals died out long, long ago. They're all extinct. In Parabolus' day, when Parabolus was king, we ate each other. That has changed.'

The other Beings nodded and murmured, thankfully.

'Well,' Lenny said, 'I'm not a cannibal, but I like meat. If you don't have it, you don't have it. I like a sausage, or a curry goat . . .'

The Beings looked blank. Lenny decided that to

34

talk about Jamaican food would be a waste of time. He was in their world, they could not understand.

'If you don't have it, you don't have it,' he repeated cheerfully, and reached for a bowl of leaves. Vi would understand, but Vi was nowhere to be seen. He chewed a leaf and smiled, trying to be brave.

Later, Daroo showed him the mat where he would sleep. He was to share a cubicle with Lilas, one of the Beings. This one appeared to be female, by her shape and by her gown. But she had horns. Lenny decided that sharing with a female was not a problem. Lilas didn't seem to mind either, looking kindly and murmuring a welcome.

Later still, Daroo and Lenny walked out towards the Unknown. At a distance, the Edge seemed clear and solid, but the closer they got the less distinct it was. What had seemed a wall of darkness became only a dim mist, thickening into the distance.

Daroo showed him a look-out post, and explained that Lenny was to take his turn on guard. The ground had been hollowed out and a wall built round it to protect the post. Daroo showed him a panel in the wall with a single red button.

'If you see something coming out of the Unknown, something you can't explain, something that might be dangerous, you press the button.'

'Something like what?'

'Something dangerous,' Daroo repeated. 'It's your job to decide. When you get tired, someone else will come to relieve you.'

'Okay, fine, no problem,' said Lenny confidently, but he didn't feel at all confident.

Daroo nodded in a friendly fashion, and bid him goodbye. With a sinking heart, Lenny watched him going away towards the shelter, his tall, slim figure silhouetted against the light of the Known. He grew smaller, and disappeared.

Lenny turned to watch the darkness. In the mist, he began to see shapes, indistinguishable shapes, flickering flames like campfires or small volcanoes, solid objects like rocky crags or the skeletons of giants, crawling shapes, and flying shapes like birds or bats with human faces. They seemed to swarm just at the limit of his vision. Lenny closed his eyes a moment, opened them, and there was nothing but the mist. He decided he had to have a system for looking at the dark. It was no use staring straight ahead, trying to see as far as possible. His eyes worked better if he changed focus, looking far, then near, then left, then right, and tried to spot whatever could be spotted.

'Hi,' a voice said, 'how you doin', man?'

Lenny looked up to see a child sitting on the wall of his look-out post, eating a chicken leg. It was a boy, with a sort of human face, brown hair, blue eyes, white skin.

'How you doin'?' the person said again.

'Where'd you come from?' Lenny replied.

The boy gestured with the chicken bone towards the Unknown.

'Over yonder,' the boy said, and added, 'This is how they treat you? Send you out to risk your life on an empty stomach?'

Lenny looked down at the red danger button.

The boy smiled, and threw away the chicken bone. Then he rose, and walked towards the black mist. He turned once, gesturing to Lenny to follow him, and then he faded out of sight.

Lenny stared after him. That was a boy like himself. He didn't have horns, or hair on his face, and he had chicken. Somewhere in the great Unknown someone was frying chicken. He should be on that boy's side, not with the Beings, he thought. Then he remembered, he had brought trouble on the Beings once before by believing things. They had forgiven him, and trusted him enough to make him a guard, a look-out. He couldn't throw all that away for the sake of a chicken leg.

After a while, Daroo returned, bringing him a bottle of water and a handful of beans. Lenny set about eating the beans, one by one, and sipping the water.

'Did you see anything?' Daroo inquired.

'Not dangerous.'

'What did you see?'

'A boy, like myself. A white boy.'

'A white boy!'

'Yes,' said Lenny, 'nothing strange about that.

You Beings are all black, but where I come from, we have all colours, black, white, yellow, in between. Different colours, but all the same, more or less.'

'Did the boy speak?'

'He was eating a chicken leg, and just before he walked back into the Unknown he threw the bone away, over there.'

'There are no chickens left.'

'How do you know?' Lenny said. 'It stands to reason, if all that is unknown, there could be chickens there.'

'Logically, my friend Lenny, you are right. Let's search for the chicken bone.'

Lenny was pleased at having won the argument, and even more pleased that Daroo had called him friend, but something told him he wouldn't find the bone.

'Never mind,' he said, 'never mind. But tell me something else, Daroo. If there are no chickens, how do you know what a chicken is? How come?'

'In former days there were chickens. In former days ...'

'In Parabolus' day?'

'... chickens, and other animals, and trees. We were all greedy. We cut down all the trees and ate all the animals. We turned the mountains into desert. We fought wars, war after war after war.'

'What about?'

'Oh, anything,' Daroo said, 'anything at all. One time there was a war about whether God wore shoes to walk the sky, or went around barefoot.'

'Who won?' Lenny said.

'Nobody. Nobody ever wins a war.'

Daroo relieved Lenny of his post, and he returned to the shelter. When the gloom came, he lay on his mat, with Lilas curled up on hers on the other side of the cubicle. Lenny couldn't sleep. He was thinking of the chicken bone, and whether God wore shoes. He looked across at Lilas, curled up, sleeping, and he thought of his sister, Vi.

Poor Vi. Where was she?

The Flying Wheelchair

Vi was doing fine. With her quick intelligence and sense of fun, she soon endeared herself to Oompallah. She told the Princess of the Beings funny stories of escapades in Kingston, Jamaica, like the time she and Lenny put Moses' goat in Granny's bedroom, and Oompallah told her the history of the planet Knos. Vi did tricks like turning cartwheels, and sang Bob Marley songs; and Oompallah told her how the Beings looked after their planet. No Being had too much of anything, and no Being went without. A Being was allowed to be born only when another Being died, as there were only so many souls, and each Being had to have one.

The Beings had no money, Oompallah explained. No Being was rich, and no Being was allowed to be poor. The biggest sin on the planet Knos was to be greedy. Parabolus had been greedy, always wanting more, more, more, and that was how he had nearly destroyed the planet, used up all the animals and trees, and why he had to be locked up in the rock.

Vi was impressed; she thought it all made sense, and she liked Oompallah, if only she wasn't quite so solemn, quite so good, quite so careful, and

40

quite so loving. She wanted to see her vexed, or quarrelsome, or even in tears. She would have seemed more human. In turn, Oompallah adored Vi, as if the little girl, hopping on one leg, laughing, pretending to be fierce or frightening, as if she were a pet kitten rolling a ball of string around Oompallah's palace.

There was a part of the crystal city Vi was not allowed to enter. These were the rooms of Queen Asmara, the mother of Oompallah, and also the mother of Parabolus. Asmara was fond of her good daughter, but to tell the truth she also had a soft spot for her wicked son. For that reason, she wasn't allowed to rule the planet any more, but she was given the best rooms in the palace, all the food she could eat, and everybody respected her and said, 'Yes, Queen Asmara, yes ma'am, you're absolutely right, ma'am.' They said that whether they meant it or not, even though Beings weren't supposed to lie.

Vi wasn't allowed to see Queen Asmara, in case the shock of seeing the mischievous little human was too much for the old queen.

Nobody had reckoned on reggae.

Vi had joined a singing class, trying to learn Being music. Being voices have enormous range, from grumbling bass to a treble too high for the human ear, and their harmonies were so complicated Vi couldn't follow them. A Being chorus sounded to her like seventeen church choirs and a rat bat, all singing a different song at the same

41

time.

Vi decided to liven it up a bit, and make it simple. She improvised a steel drum out of a cooking pot, she sang, and she danced to her own kind of music. The Beings picked it up right away, and joined in to please her. Pretty soon, the great hall was full of dancing Beings, shaking their shoulders and their hips, jumping up and down and clashing horns, and singing 'Every little thing is going to be all right.'

They were making so much noise they woke Asmara who had just settled down for her after-noon nap. The queen called for her flying wheel-chair, and flew around the palace until she spotted the source of the noise.

The great hall looked like a street party, the Beings hopping up and down and shaking, and this little human girl leading them, beating a rhythm on a cooking pot. Asmara's bleary eyes went wide with shock. With reggae ringing in her ears she flew away in search of Oompallah, and found her in her private room reading the Book of Knos.

'Oompallah,' Asmara said, her nostrils twitch-ing, 'there is a wicked thing in the city.'

'Yes, mother, yes,' Oompallah said, not believing her, knowing that Asmara tended to be excitable.

' "Yes, mother yes." Why do you say it in that tone of voice? You don't believe me?'

Oompallah didn't, but she decided to be care-ful. With Parabolus out of the rock anything could happen. Her mother might be telling the truth after all.

'Mother dear, certainly I believe you think there is a wicked thing in the city. Have you seen it?'

'With my own eyes.'

'Tell.'

'It looks like a very small Being, but it has a different head, smooth skin, and no horns. It has bewitched the Beings and made them dance and sing, not to some proper music, but to some dreadful, mindless noise.'

'That's reggae,' said Oompallah, 'and the little girl's name is Vi.'

'You've seen her too?'

'Yes, she's been here for some time. She and her brother landed here, on Knos. They came from another star, a place called Jamaica.'

Asmara put a hand to her heart, which was thumping dangerously, and sat back in her chair.

'You believe that?'

'Yes.'

'How did they come?' Asmara demanded. 'In some sort of flying machine?'

'No. They travelled on the attraction of the stars.'

'Where did they land?'

'First on the Layer of Dust, then in the Green Gully. We found them by the Rock of Parabolus. They, being children, were deceived by him, and they let him go.'

Asmara's heart was really thumping now. Her

beloved son was free, but that meant trouble.

'That's what they told you? If you believe that you'll believe anything. Parabolus must have freed himself, and sent the little girl as a spy. She is a wickedness!'

'I like her,' Oompallah said.

This was too much for the ancient Being. She uttered a strangled cry, and slid, clutching at her chest, out of her chair. She crashed to the floor and lay still, her eyes open, and her tongue sticking out. Beings were summoned who picked her up tenderly and carried her back to her room, where she was put to bed, and where she lay for days hovering between life and death.

Eventually she decided to come back to life, as she couldn't get her own way if she were dead. Oompallah, her loving daughter, came to see her as soon as Asmara regained consciousness. She held her hand and comforted her. Asmara did not want to be comforted, not while Vi was in the city singing and dancing and spreading corruption among the Beings, but Oompallah's faith in Vi was just as firm as her mother's conviction of her wickedness.

Beings are supposed to see each other's point of view, and find a fair and friendly outcome to every argument. So when Asmara suggested that Vi should be brought to trial, Oompallah, knowing she was innocent, agreed. Guards were sent for Vi, who found her being very good indeed. She was with a wise old Being, trying to learn the language of Knos. This isn't easy as it is written not in words but in colours, numbers, and musical notes. Vi was suffering from brain strain, and she was almost glad when the Guards came and arrested her, and led her away for trial.

There were six judges behind a high table, three male Beings and three female Beings, all extremely solemn. Oompallah sat in the middle of them to make the odd number. Asmara buzzed about in her flying chair.

Vi had no idea what was going on, and stood in front of the judges, pigeon-toed and hands behind her back, twisting her blue sash.

'Hello,' she said. 'Peace.'

'Are you an agent of Parabolus?' Asmara snapped, pointing one of her three fingers at the little girl.

Vi was amazed, so surprised she did not know what to say. This horrible old thing was accusing her of something, she thought.

Vi had forgotten that the Beings could read her thoughts.

Asmara smiled. 'I'm not accusing you, I only want the truth. Beings are forgiving.'

Oh good, Vi thought, then I'll be all right.

'Yes, you'll be all right,' Oompallah said kindly. 'Just answer the questions.'

'What do you want to know?' Vi said, out loud.

'What is Parabolus' plan?' Asmara asked. 'What wickedness is the boy up to, and why did he send you here?'

45

The one in the wheelchair is mad, Vi thought, stark, staring.

Asmara sniffed. 'I can hear you. I know what you're thinking, you wicked little thing.' She turned to the judges, 'What shall we do with her?'

'I don't know what you think I did, but it's not true,' Vi said out loud.

'You were dancing and singing reggae!'

'I only wanted to be jolly.'

'That's the first step to wickedness.'

Oh help, Vi thought. Oh Lenny, where are you?

'If you admit your wickedness,' Asmara said, all smooth and kind, 'then we can have mercy on you.'

'I'm not wicked! I'm not wicked!' Vi shouted.

'Do you want things you cannot have?' asked one of the judges.

'Who doesn't?' Vi said.

'Do you think you're clever?' asked another.

Not clever enough to get out of this one, Vi thought.

'Are you greedy?'

'Yes and no,' Vi said.

'Are you angry?'

'Yes, I am!'

'Do you want to do violent things?' Asmara asked, coming close to her.

'Yes, yes, I want to strangle you!' Vi shouted out loud. 'Parabolus was right! He's the good guy! You're the bad guys!'

'What, what?'

'Parabolus was right! You're the bad guys! You locked him up, and now you want to lock me up. I hate you, I hate you, I hate you!'

Asmara drew herself up to her full height, which wasn't much, and spoke calmly.

'Beings do not hate. Beings are tolerant and kind, forgiving and sharing. You are a wicked thing! Guards, take her away!'

Vi looked imploringly at Oompallah, her friend, her only hope. But Oompallah's face was grave. Vi had condemned herself by saying Parabolus was right. Still, the princess tried to save her little friend.

'Vi didn't mean it,' she said to the judges. 'She didn't really mean it, she was just frightened.'

Asmara would have none of that. 'If she didn't mean it, she showed she has no judgement, and no self-control. She has not learned to control her anger and her envy. A period of correction is required. Sentence her, Oompallah!'

Oompallah sighed. 'I will be lenient,' she said, 'Only a thousand years. Put her in the cavern underneath my throne.'

Poor Vi.

Journey into the Unknown

There was something going on in the Unknown. Daroo was sure of it. Lenny, coming off watch, had reported unusual activity. He had sighted a column of what looked like giant alligators proceeding slowly through the dark mist. There had been fountains of fire, rising and falling. Yellow balls of light had swooped and swung, and whizzed towards Lenny as he crouched in his post, coming like lightning, stopping dead, and returning just as fast into the dark Unknown. There had been a wailing sound like screech owls calling in a chorus, a rattling, rolling noise like thunder overhead. Then the stink came, creeping out of the mist, a stench of rotting, like rats drowning in a cesspit.

It was the stink that sent Lenny running back from the outpost, bounding over the ground to the protection of the shelter.

'Daroo, Daroo, the place has gone mad, man! Parabolus must be giving a party.'

Daroo called a council of the Beings. They gathered in an informal group, some sitting, some standing, one cross-legged, one with an arm around another, and even one lying on her stomach, scratching pictures on the floor.

'What are we going to do?'

'Send word to Oompallah.'

'But we don't know what to say.'

'Say something's happened.'

'Something like what?'

'We should send word that there is unusual activity in the Unknown, the meaning of which we cannot yet discern. At the same time, we should try to find out what it is.'

'How can we do that?'

'We watch and wait.'

'That's not good enough. We must send an expedition to find out what is going on.'

There was silence among the Beings. The thought of such an expedition was enough to make the brave stop breathing for a while.

'No one has travelled the Unknown.'

'Not true. Some have entered it, but no one has returned.'

'Is it the only way?'

'It is the best. If there is danger, the city must be warned.'

'Who will go?'

'We can draw lots.'

'This is too serious for eeny-meeny-mo.'

'We must volunteer.'

'How many shall we send?'

'Three.'

'Three is a magic number.'

There was a pause while each Being weighed his bravery against his cowardice, his comfort against danger, his love of life against his fear of death.

'I will go,' Daroo said.

'And I, said Lilas, the female Being, who seemed so easygoing.

'Me three,' said Lenny.

Daroo looked gravely at him, his large luminous eyes filled with love.

'No, Lenny, no. You're not even a Being. Why should you risk your life?'

'You are my friend,' Lenny said. 'So I want to go with you.'

'No.'

'What's more, if I don't go I'll always be sorry.'

'No.'

'What's more, I'm the only one with nothing to lose. I'll never go home again.'

Lilas leaned over Lenny, lowered her slim, horned head, and with a gentle muzzle kissed the top of his head.

'You're home here,' she said. 'Let him come with us, Daroo. Because he is different, he may see what we don't see, he may understand what we don't understand.'

It was agreed.

* * *

They started on the flying pogo-sticks, quite low, and moving cautiously in the mist. But before long, and quite suddenly, the anti-gravity engines which powered the sticks ceased to function, and the three scouts fell to the ground. Where they landed the surface varied with every step. Sometimes it was firm, sometimes as thin as water, and in the darkness of the Unknown it was hard to tell which was which.

Daroo, Lenny, and Lilas roped themselves together like mountain climbers, so if one fell the other two could act as rescuers. They walked on, pausing to look and listen. But with their arrival all activity had ceased. There was no sign of giant reptiles, of fiery fountains or revolving lights, nothing but an eerie silence.

The silence was frightening because it told them, truthfully or not, that their arrival had been noticed, that something in the Unknown was watching them.

Clear of the swampy substance, they found a loose, hard surface which rustled as they moved through it, like fallen leaves. The further they went the thicker it grew, and the louder the rustling, until they were wading up to their knees. As Lenny was the smallest he would be the first to disappear, which worried him. He scooped up some of the surface in his hand to look at it. It was alive! It was composed of insects, and the rustling sound had not been footsteps but the beating of a million wings and the scratching of a million legs.

'I vote we turn back,' said Lenny. 'If these things start to bite, we're past history.'

'Eat them,' replied Daroo, stuffing a handful in his mouth and munching happily.

That was a signal for the insects to depart, rising around them in a swirling cloud, settling on one

51

direction, and departing in a roar of wings, leaving the explorers on a barren rock.

'Let's talk,' Daroo said, 'and decide what next to do.'

Lilas and Lenny loosened the packs they carried, loaded with food and water, and set them down.

'So where are we?' Lenny asked.

'I don't know,' Daroo replied.

'Do we know the way back?'

'No.'

'We've seen nothing.'

'And heard nothing.'

'I think they're watching us.'

'Who?'

'Mysterious creatures.'

'What would happen if we separated?'

'We'd die alone.'

'I still think that we should separate,' Lenny said. 'I'll tell you why. I am the one, me and Vi, that set Parabolus free. If he's going to make himself known, he's going to speak to me. I did him a favour, right? So I can ask a favour of him.'

'Parabolus takes, he does not give.'

'We'll see about that,' Lenny said, making up his mind. He removed the rope that tied him to his friends.

'Wait here,' he said, heroically, 'I'll be right back.'

'How will you find us?' Daroo asked.

'I will.'

'Good luck,' said Lilas, lovingly.

Lenny started walking in the dark, not knowing where he was going, or the way back. Then he had an idea. Reaching into his pack he took out a bag of white beans that was part of their rations. Every ten paces that he took he dropped a bean, making a trail of pale dots on the ground. He walked on through the black mist for what seemed like hours, but was probably only minutes. Then suddenly he heard a sound that made his blood run cold.

It was Vi's voice, calling for help. It sounded quite close, just over the rim of rock to his right. The voice was strained, high, and desperate, as if Vi had been calling for a long time, and lost all hope of rescue.

'Help, Lenny, help me . . . !'

Lenny ran towards the rock-rim, the voice louder as he ran, but something warned him to be careful, a memory of disappearing lizards, of a boy with a chicken bone, and all the mystery of this unknown world. He stopped. Then he moved forward again more cautiously, crawling, or on all fours, until he could look over the rock-rim.

Below, in an obscure hollow, there were shapes moving around a fire which came out of the ground. In the fire was the giant shape of Parabolus himself, some ten feet tall, dressed in a tattered shroud, his pale face greasy, his long, lank hair down to his shoulders. It was he, calling in Vi's voice.

'Help, Lenny, help, help me, help me . . . !'

Lenny looked, but did not move. Parabolus

53

laughed, as if he knew his call was being resisted. He walked calmly through the fire, and moved among the grotesque shapes surrounding him. Somehow they reminded Lenny of humans, of all races and colours, but humans they were not. One with blond hair and a bloody mouth was the colour of a shark's belly, another a black blob with waving spikes, a third looked like a bullfrog with slimy, bulging eyes, and a fourth was merely a shape of feathers, changing all the time, wings beating inward towards an open throat. Parabolus walked through them, calling them by name. Lazy, Spite, Greed and Vexatiousness. They laughed with pleasure to be recognized, and purred like pets.

Lenny kept watching as Parabolus returned to the fire, stepping on it as if mounting a pulpit, and began to preach to his obscene congregation. Lenny listened as Parabolus reminded them of troubles, their imprisonment, their hunger, and their suffering. He swore that all the Beings would be killed, and he would rule again. They would feast, they would revel, they would do whatever they wanted, to whomever they wanted, and whenever they wanted. There would be no reckoning, no price to pay. Desire would rule. Knos would be theirs again to make them rich and give them pleasure.

The monsters stamped and cheered. Parabolus silenced them, and looked towards the rock-rim.

'Lenny!' he called, in Vi's sweet voice. 'Lenny, dem lock me up! You don't believe me? True as truth, cross my heart and hope to die, dem lock me in a dungeon for a thousand years! Go to Parabolus, Lenny, for he alone can help us.'

It must be true, Lenny thought, it must be. Nobody could imitate Vi so perfectly. She was using Parabolus to speak for her in the same way Parabolus had used him, Lenny, when he was imprisoned in the rock. Whatever he thought about the Beings, whatever loyalty he had to them, Vi came first, and he must go to her.

Lenny stood up, and started towards the fire. Strong hands seized him from behind, strong arms picked him up, and held him. He was pinned against a strong chest and a beating heart. Looking up, he saw Daroo's face, his soft eyes, his curling horns, and ceased to struggle. Swiftly, carrying Lenny, Daroo ran back along the path of beans towards the frontier of the Known.

Vi in the Dungeon

Vi was feeling sorry for herself. She was completely unaware that Parabolus had borrowed her voice. She herself had no use for it. She was locked up in a dungeon with no one to talk to, and nothing to do. So, she thought, I'll have to think of something.

First, she could get to know the place. It was about eight feet wide and ten feet long. The floor was stone, worn smooth by previous prisoners. The walls were rock, and still uneven. She had been bundled into her prison, kicking and screaming about goodies and baddies, so she hadn't had time to see how the door worked. It wasn't a proper door but a rolling stone, that is, a solid stone cartwheel which moved in a groove in the rock. It could be pushed aside from outside, but from the inside it was immovable.

At the other end the dungeon narrowed to a point, where a crack in the rock led nowhere. Some of the water that tasted like coconut dripped from the rock above and trickled away through a hole in the floor. There was another hole in the roof about nine inches square, covered with a metal grille, and too small anyway, even for a little girl. Every once in a while a tiny basket of salad and fruit was lowered on a string, then lifted away again, and the metal grille replaced. There was a stone shelf for sleeping, with a plastic lilo.

Even a mouse would have been company, but there was no mouse.

Vi guessed that the hole in the roof came out in the floor of the great hall. She remembered that Oompallah had said 'in the cavern under my throne'.

She had also said, 'a thousand years'. How long was that? How many lifetimes? She divided a thousand by threescore and ten. She didn't like the answer. But doing mathematics was a way of passing the time. If, Vi thought, if she had been there three days, two hours and fifty minutes, how much time did she have left? She did that one in a flash. Teacher would have been proud. Then she thought of a harder one. If a thousand years is a hundred, what percentage of a hundred is three days, two hours, and fifty-five minutes? That one took longer, because she had nothing to write with, and she had trouble with all those noughts after the decimal point. It was a very small percentage indeed.

'But!' Vi said to herself, out loud, getting her voice back, 'But ... the year on Knos is different, the day is a different length, and the minute is a different minute, so a thousand years is not a thousand years. So I can't work out how long I've been here, how long I'm going to be here, and what percentage of my sentence I have served.'

57

She began to feel miserable.

'Vi!' Oompallah's voice echoed in the cavern.

Vi looked up. Oompallah must be sitting on her throne, or somewhere up there, not far away.

'Yes? Are you talking to me?'

'Are you sorry yet?'

'Sorry for what?'

'For being rude to my mother, and for shouting at the court.'

'Yes, I'm sorry.'

'Truly?'

'Yes, I'm sorry because I got locked up, but I'm not sorry for what I said.'

'You're going to be down there a long time.'

'I don't care! You can punish me, but you can't make me change my mind!' Vi shouted, kicking at the rock.

'Listen to reason,' Oompallah said sweetly through the hole in the roof. 'You were found where Parabolus escaped. You can't blame my mother for thinking you're on his side.'

'She's stupid,' Vi muttered.

'And you were behaving differently from the Beings, and encouraging them to follow you.'

'They were having fun.'

'That's neither here nor there,' Oompallah said, firmly. 'We've found out that some things you enjoy are good for you, and good for everybody, and some things lead to wickedness. Beings have learned you must avoid the things that lead to wickedness.'

'But everybody likes things like that.'

'Yes, even I,' Oompallah said, trying to be fair. 'There is wickedness in all of us, spite, greed, and vexatiousness, pleasure in cruelty, pleasure in someone else's pain.'

'All I was doing was singing and dancing.'

'Asmara thought it was wicked.'

'Asmara was wrong.'

'She is right about one thing. Wickedness must be locked away.'

'I get it,' Vi said, 'I'm not stupid. When you locked up your brother Parabolus, you thought you'd locked up all the wickedness.'

'Yes, clever girl, you understand.'

'But, but, but,' Vi said, 'but isn't there any good in him? There must be good in him.'

'No,' Oompallah replied, definite as can be. 'Parabolus is totally, utterly wicked.'

'Is there anybody who is totally good?'

'Yes, the Great Being, whose name is written in the Book of Knos.'

'You mean the name that sounds like music?'

'Yes,' came Oompallah's voice, reverently, 'the name that sounds like music.'

'So okay,' Vi said, 'the Great Being is good, right, but he lets wicked things happen. Why can't you allow a little wickedness?'

'I'm sorry, Vi, you're just a little girl, and you can't possibly understand these things.'

'That's what they all say when they don't know the answer.'

59

Oompallah went away, and Vi sat down on the stone floor. Her brain was tired. She couldn't argue with Oompallah any more. Words were words, but she was still locked up, and for a thousand years. Words would not get her out. She looked at the hole in the roof, and shouted.

'You can lock me up, but you cannot change my mind! Your mother is an old bat!'

The Mountain Beings

'From what I heard,' Lenny was saying, 'trouble is coming. I didn't make out any definite plans, but Parabolus was talking war.'

'When?'

'Must be soon.'

They were having a conference of the Beings in the shelter, and the scouts were reporting what they had done and seen.

'What weapons does he have?'

'Couldn't tell you. Terrible things.'

'We must report back to the city.'

'We've done that already, and warned Oompallah to prepare to defend herself.'

'How did you do that?' Lenny asked.

'Do what?'

'Report back?'

'By radio.'

'You have radios?'

'Yes.'

'Just like the ones on earth!'

'They must be,' Daroo said, who liked to explain things. 'The radio waves are the same throughout the universe. The forms of life may be different, but the radios will be the same.'

'So I can call up on the radio, and find out how

Vi is getting on?'

There was an embarrassment among the Beings.
Lenny looked from one to the other trying to
understand. There was a sadness in the way they
held their lovely heads, and they would not look at
him.

'How is Vi?' he repeated, and again had no
answer. 'You mean Parabolus was right? She is
locked up?'

'For her own good,' a Being said, 'and for the
good of all.'

'Which is the same thing,' said another, and they
all nodded in agreement.

Lenny was vexed, really vexed. Vi was locked up,
and they were solemnly sitting there giving him
lessons in morality!

'It's your war, not mine. Count me out!' he said
defiantly, 'I'm not going to be a hero, I'm leaving.
I'm going to look for Vi.'

He jumped up and headed for the door, seizing
his pogo-stick from the rack where they were kept.

'I hope Parabolus kills you all,' he said, and
wished he hadn't said it.

'Is your engine charged? Lenny! You'll crash!'
Daroo called after him, but Lenny had not heard.
He was already outside, and had already stepped
on to the silver disc, pulled back on the stick and
taken to the air.

Behind him, and below, lay the darkness of the
Unknown, the small blob that was the shelter, and
in front of him the barren mountain range that lay

between him and the crystal city. He had to get high enough to clear those mountains and leaned on the stick to do so. It responded, but sluggishly, as if unwilling to fly that high, or fly alone. Judging he had the height, he pushed forward to get more speed, and the mountains rushed towards him.

He could see the craggy peaks and the deep valleys, cliffs and jagged pinnacles reaching up to grab him. He was almost over the mountains at their highest and wildest when the pogo-stick began to fail. He could feel the power draining out of it, and the speed lessening. He was losing height. The wall of rock loomed up in front of him, and knowing he could not clear it Lenny circled, getting lower and lower, down into the deep blue shadows below the peaks, down, down, down on the ever-weakening stick, looking for some place to land. He passed between two mountains, cleft by a narrow canyon, and entered a hidden valley.

There he saw, miracle of miracles, trees, not only trees but tiny fields, a meadow, and a mountain stream, and huts, small round huts grouped in a little village. Lenny landed on the meadow, using his last drop of power to settle softly on the grass.

He looked up at the peaks around him, and above them he saw a blue, blue sky, a bowl of sky, and a little orange sun.

Had he come back to earth? There were animals grazing in the field. They weren't sheep, and they weren't goats, but they had four legs, a head and a tail. As he walked towards the village, a birdlike creature sang, and he thought he heard a dog bark and a rooster crow. He saw Beings, female, washing in the stream, Beings, male, digging in the fields, and smaller Beings carrying water and tending herds. It was like days gone by, and it made him feel at ease. He walked confidently into the middle of the village, where the huts formed a rough circle and the ground was beaten hard and flat, and called out:

'Oi! Oi! Anybody there? I'm Lenny.'

Beings, scruffy-looking ones, with patched clothes and hard hands, Beings with long knives, came out of the huts and surrounded him.

'I'm Lenny,' he said, 'Peace and Love.'

They approached him cautiously, knives at the ready. Perhaps they had never seen a strange Being in their lives, much less a man, or, in this case, a boy.

'I crashed,' Lenny said. 'I fell.' He made signs to show he had come out of the sky. Then he smiled and put out his hands to show he was unarmed, and waited.

They watched him, and he stood in the circle of eyes, of horny hands, of knives, of sinewy labour-hardened bodies, and waited.

One of them came forward, and touched him. That broke the tension, and the Being turned to the others, assuring them that Lenny was real, and small, and harmless. Then they all started talking at once, guessing at what he was, at where he came from, and wondering what to do with him. They decided to feed him first, and make him welcome.

They ate in the largest of the huts, all squatting on the floor around a large dish into which they dipped their fingers. Lenny was the guest, so he had the first dip. An ancient Being followed him, and then all the other males, and the females waited quietly around the wall. The dish was piled high with grains like corn, and the roast carcass of one of the animals he had seen grazing. In another dish were tiny fish from the stream and in another, fruit, and something that looked and smelled like cheese.

They ate, burping and smiling, and when full they all fell silent. The dish was carried away for the females to have their share. Lenny remained with the males, not sure whether to speak or be spoken to.

'Thank you,' he said to the ancient Being, 'thank you.'

The Old One nodded.

'Thanks to everybody,' Lenny said, remembering his manners, 'and thanks to the cook.'

The Old One nodded.

'They told me in the city that there were no trees left, and no animals.'

'The mountains hide us,' the Old One said, and nodded, and all the others nodded with him, as Beings do.

'Do you go to the city?'

The Old One shook his head.

'Do they come here?'

'No. We are hidden in the mountains.'

'Have you always lived here?'

'We found this place, in flight. Long ago, we lived on the plains, and in the old days we multiplied and prospered. Then came the great war when Parabolus was driven out, and the Princess Oompallah took control. She made too many rules. Everything was in order, everything in its place. So many Beings per square foot, so much food for each Being, and so much happiness before you died. We weren't allowed to quarrel, or to fight.'

'Wasn't that good?' Lenny asked.

'Yes, that was good, but something was missing, something called freedom. So we left, and came to the mountains. We don't ask the mountains to make us rich, and we don't tell the mountains what to do. We only live and die in their great company.'

'Suppose you find gold,' Lenny said.

'Let's hope we don't,' the Old One said, and all the Beings nodded.

'But there are wonderful things in the city,' Lenny said, showing off his knowledge. 'They have flying machines and vision screens. They have machines for planting and for reaping, for building and for tearing down. They have music, dancing, funny jokes, and machines do all the work. Wouldn't you like machines to do your work?'

66

'No,' the Old One said, 'working is living.'

The other Beings were doing that nodding again, agreeing with him.

'Beings are fools,' he added, 'to let machines do the living for them.'

Lenny was not quite sure about this, so he decided to change the subject.

'In the city, they say it was wrong to eat animals.'

'We love our animals, so we want to eat them. We give them life, we look after them. They give life back to us. The trees give life, we give it back to them. Even the corn that passes through us goes back to the cornfield. Here in the mountains, when a Being dies, he is buried, and a tree is planted where he lies. Each tree in the valley is the new life of a Being.'

'Well,' Lenny said, 'that's very interesting, but I must move on. I mean, thanks for the food and everything, but I must go.'

'You don't like the way we live?'

'I like it, yes. It sounds great, but ...'

'I told you all those things so you would want to stay with us.'

'Yes, I would, yes,' Lenny stuttered, 'but there's my sister, Vi. I have to find my sister Vi.'

'Your sister must look after herself.'

'She can't. She's useless. She can't even tie her own shoelaces.'

'We will not let you go,' the Old One said.

Lenny was worried. The old Being said that as if he meant it.

67

'Why not?' Lenny asked.

'If you leave, you will tell them where we are. They will come and steal our animals, and cut down all our trees.'

'I won't tell them,' Lenny said, 'I promise. If you let me leave I'll never ever say to anybody "there are some happy Beings hidden in the mountains and they've got animals and trees!" No, I'd never say that. Promise, promise, promise.'

The Old One thought about it for a while.

'You say that now, but you may not be able to keep your promise, it may just slip out. No, we will have to kill you. Tomorrow, you can choose a place to lie, and the kind of tree you want to grow over your head.'

'You mean I'm going to die tomorrow?'

'Unless you decide to stay with us forever.'

'Tomorrow! Can I think about it tonight?'

While the others slept, Lenny did some serious pondering. If he were a hero, and stuck to his guns, he was a dead hero. But if he agreed to stay, he might find a way of escape. So, in the morning, he was all smiles. He'd thought about it, he said. He'd like to stay. He would really! He thought they had the secret, a simple life in harmony with nature, loving their animals and trees, living cheerfully, and dying peacefully without regret. Yes, he'd like to stay, and could he have a job?

They said he could carry the night soil, and spread it on the fields.

Lenny said fine, okay, right, that's what he'd do.

It was a worthwhile job, and he'd be pleased to do it. Every morning he collected the night soil of the village into buckets, and every day he spread it on the fields as fertilizer. Then every evening he swam in the stream to wash off, in the clear, cold mountain water. At night he ate with the Beings, and listened to them sing songs and tell stories. He was happy enough, but he couldn't forget Vi.

By the pool where he swam, where the water was deep and still, there were plants that looked like bulrushes, with long, thick fibrous stems and plumed tops. Every day he would break one off and hide it. The bulrushes grew so fast that the Beings didn't notice. When the rushes were dry, Lenny began to weave. He didn't know how, but he thought this might be a good time to learn. First his weave was too tight, then too loose, then too crooked, then too straight, but he got the hang of it in the end. He made a large, shallow, circular basket, big enough for a boy to sit in. This he put back in the water, which made the dry rushes swell, so the water itself made the basket waterproof.

One day, after his swim, he climbed into it, pushed off into the middle of the stream, and floated down. He had no way of steering, so he trusted to the current to carry him down and away.

The pleasant valley and the high peaks glided past. Sitting in his bulrush basket he saw the village receding into the distance, the fields like handkerchiefs, the animals like dots, the trees like smudges on the mountain walls. Then he entered a narrow gorge where the stream grew swifter, carrying the spinning basket helter-skelter down. Lenny hung on for dear life as the water spouted round him, and the dark cliffs loomed over him. Then he heard the thunder of a waterfall, and his basket was slung out into the air as the water disappeared beneath him. He sailed, like a sombrero in a hurricane, carried on the wind, balancing the basket so he did not tip. Lenny descended, spinning, through the thin blue air, through mists, through spray, and landed, skidding on a down-slope, sliding, sliding, sliding more slowly till he came to rest, cotched between boulders, his basket bent upwards like a curling leaf.

He stepped out, and was so dizzy he fell down, and lay there for a while.

When he recovered, he rose, and found himself on the edge of the great plain which led to the crystal city. In the fields the machines went to and fro, back and forth in automatic motion, so the plain looked like the insides of a giant clock stretched out before him. There were no Beings visible.

Lenny noticed that while most machines stayed in the field they worked in, going back and forth, others, carrying crops, moved towards the city. He had only to hop on board, and hop from one to the other, or find one going all the way, to cross the plain and reach the city, and find Vi.

Easy.

Escape to Danger

Vi was still there, in her dungeon. She had given up hope of seeing Lenny again, and given up hope of getting out. Mathematics no longer seemed a useful way of passing the time, so she had taken up painting. She had read in school that rock paintings in caves were one of the earliest signs of civilization on Earth, and she had seen pictures of Egyptian tombs, in which the drawings were all flat, without perspective, but very beautiful none the less. She thought she'd try to do something like that, to leave a record of her imprisonment. It would be better than writing 'Vi was here' or playing tic-tac-toe on the wall with a sharp stone.

Every day, her food was lowered to her in a basket. She saved the fruit and berries, and the leaves of a purple salad plant, and oil. She dried the berries, and pressed them. She mixed the juice with the oil and with powdered rock she took from the wall. In the end, she had two colours, a rusty sort of red, and a bluey-green.

With these, she set to work to do a comic strip around the walls called 'The History of Vi'. It showed Granny's house, children sleeping on the roof, voyages among the stars, landing on Knos, Parabolus and the Beings, and then ...

She was trying to paint the crystal city when she heard a series of sharp reports like firecrackers at Christmas, and then louder noises, like doors banging, and cars crashing into one another. The walls of the dungeon trembled, and the floor moved.

'Oh my goodness,' Vi said out loud, 'it's an earthquake, and I'm going to be buried alive!'

She sat in a corner with her knees drawn up, her hands over her ears, and her eyes shut. Little showers of dust rained down on her from the roof of the dungeon. Then it was quiet. Vi lifted her head, and looked around. She was still alive. Then the banging started again, and she doubled up again and squeezed her eyelids tight. She thought of beautiful things like the rag doll she had when she was six, who had lost one eye, but who was most everlastingly beloved.

Then it was quiet again, followed by the sound of many feet, coming into the hall above her head. Vi had practised making sense of sounds, and she calculated that the Beings were gathering for some sort of emergency conference. The noise of the feet grew, and then was overtaken by the twittering and grumbling of excited conversation and the voice of Oompallah, silencing them.

'Beings! The terrible day has come! The thing we feared has happened! The city is under attack!'

There was general moaning, and ooh-ing and aah-ing from the assembled Beings.

'We have known, our scouts have reported, that

Parabolus and the Wicked Things have been arming in the vast Unknown, preparing to take revenge, and to reconquer Knos!'

There was another chorus of lamentation from the Beings.

Vi stopped listening. She had noticed that there was more light then usual in her dungeon. Looking round, she noticed that the crack at the far end had widened. She had thought it was an earthquake, but in view of what Oompallah had said it must have been caused by a bombardment. Anyway, the rock had shifted, and the crack opened. She examined it. There was just enough room for a small girl to climb upwards, and there was light at the top.

Scratched by the rough rock, squeezed all the time and stuck some of the time, Vi struggled upwards, choking in the dust. She reached out with her hands, found the edges of the crack, pulled herself up, and found herself in the middle of a group of Beings who were all listening to Oompallah. They were so distressed at what she was saying that they paid no attention to the sudden appearance of a bedraggled little girl rising out of the floor.

'What will become of us?' Oompallah was saying.

'We will all die,' the Beings replied, and sighed like the retreating sea.

'No! We must live!' Oompallah insisted, valiantly, 'and learn to love the Wicked Things.'

'That is worse than death,' Asmara croaked. 'I

can remember what you cannot imagine. In the days of my terrible son, there was cruelty and torture, theft and murder, every male was for himself alone, and every female was a victim.'

'Then let us die,' the Beings murmured, like a congregation praying, 'let us die.'

'We can suffer under him,' Oompallah insisted, 'and teach Parabolus the evil of his ways. We can make the Wicked understand.'

'Let us suffer,' the Beings murmured all together.

'There is good in everyone,' Oompallah went on confidently, 'we will suffer until Parabolus is good.'

'Never!' old Asmara squeaked. 'You'll waste your time. Parabolus is bad. The Wicked Things are bad, bad through and through, and rotten. When a thing is rotten, the only change is for the worse.'

'Then let us die,' the Beings repeated. 'Let us die.'

The great hall was still. The Beings all were silent. It seemed they had given up hope, and were meekly waiting for the end, like birds at nightfall tucking their heads beneath their folded wings.

All this was too much for Vi. Until then she had been making herself invisible, taking no part in their great parliament. But this was too much!

'I think you're all being stupid!' she said in her small, clear voice.

She walked through the astonished Beings, who stood aside to let her pass, until she stood beside Oompallah, and climbed the footstool of the throne.

74

'Don't mind me,' Vi said. 'I'm just a little girl, just visiting, and it's none of my business if you all want to die, but that's just stupid. You must fight!' she said and waved her little fist. 'Fight, and drive Parabolus back into the Unknown.'

'We can't fight. It's against the Rules.'

'You'll have to change the Rules,' Vi said, sharpishly.

'Change the Rules!' the Beings gasped together.

'Yes, change the Rules! Tell me something. How did you get rid of Parabolus in the first place? How did you get him locked up in the stone?'

'Asmara knows,' Oompallah said.

'I'll tell you how,' Asmara said. She'd been dying for a chance to be important again, and this was it. 'Put my chair beside the throne so every Being can hear me,' she ordered, and eager Beings lifted her and placed her between little Vi and the beautiful Oompallah.

'We fought!' she began. 'We had a real knock-down, drag-out fight! Blood and bodies everywhere! You see, before that, Parabolus and the Wicked Things ruled. Their rules said greed was everything. They said if every Being was greedy, every Being would be rich. It worked, while Knos itself, our lovely planet, was rich. It gave us all its jewels, its gold, its animals and trees, its clean air and clear water. But came the time when Knos itself, our lovely planet, when Knos itself was poor. The starving Beings armed themselves with what was left, small stones, dry sticks, anything that was

75

at hand, and rose against Parabolus!'

The Beings nodded, listening, remembering the stories they had heard, the dreadful stories of the Bad Old Days.

Asmara went on, getting excited, 'Then in the gloom of the vanished sun, we fought against the Wicked Things and drove them out! We captured Parabolus and locked him in a stone. But the Wicked Things had all the weapons. Many of us died, but after enormous sufferings, we won!'

Asmara raised her arms above her head in triumph, and the Beings cheered.

'It was at that time,' Asmara went on, 'it was at the time we won, when we inherited a planet half destroyed, and inhabited a city made of dust, it was then we drew up the Rules. Say them after me!'

The Beings recited them, reverently:

We will all share
We will not want nor take
We will all give
We shall not be angry
We will not fight
We will make peace
We will give back to Knos
    what we have taken from her
We shall not have more children
    than we have souls ...

'Well, you've broken your own rules!' Vi interrupted loudly, and the Beings politely stopped their recitation to listen to her again.

'I mean,' Vi went on, 'you haven't given back the

things you've taken from the planet. You've just built a silly city of glass, and put a lot of machines in the countryside. And then you go around looking thoughtful, loving, and kind, but you've forgotten how to dance!'

Forks of lightning and clouds of purple smoke filled the high vaulting of the hall, like an indoor thunderstorm. In it, Parabolus appeared, riding a beast that had the body of a lion, the head of a bullfrog, and the wings of a bat.

'The dancing starts again!' his gravelly voice cried. 'I will dance on all your graves!'

The horns tilted backwards as the Beings looked up at the ghastly vision. Oompallah turned to look, and Asmara also, but little Vi sat on the footstool and looked at her feet.

'I won't look,' she thought, 'I won't let him frighten me.'

'Peace, Parabolus,' Oompallah said.

'War!' Parabolus answered.

Oompallah pleaded, 'We can all live together.'

'You will die, you and Asmara. All the other Beings will be my slaves!'

Vi tugged at the hem of Oompallah's robe.

'Tell him you'll fight,' she whispered. 'The Wicked are always cowardly, so you must be brave.'

'We'll fight!' Oompallah shouted.

'We'll fight,' echoed the multitude of Beings, and repeated it, louder and louder. And as their war-cry grew Parabolus faded into smoke and disappeared.

The War Begins

While all this was going on, Lenny was crossing the plain, so he had a good view of the first attack, the one that shook Vi's dungeon and set her free.

What he saw looked like a gathering storm, a black cloud in the sky coming from the Unknown. Closer, he could distinguish separate blobs, coming fast and high, and moving with a curious up and down motion. The blobs became shapes, winged shapes, hurtling overhead. They looked like flying dinosaurs, with long snouts ending in open jaws, thick tails trailing, and fat, armoured bodies supported by leathery wings. Hanging below these creatures were scaly legs ending in claws, grasping lumps of burning lava, too heavy and too hot to hold. So, as they flew, the creatures seemed to be playing, dropping their lava bombs, swooping down and catching them before they hit the ground, then soaring upwards to continue their threatening flight towards the city.

Over the crystal city they swooped and circled, dropping the lava, not catching it this time. They zoomed upwards in celebration of the damage they had done, swooping excitedly, seeming to chatter, to congratulate each other on the smashing and the splintering of the helpless city below.

Then the creatures turned and streaked away in a long line towards the dark Unknown.

Lenny, watching them, feared for Vi's life. He jumped off the machine he was riding on, and ran fast, in great bounds, desperate to find his little sister.

Suddenly, on the road ahead, Daroo appeared, coming softly to land on his pogo-stick. Lilas was with him, and two or three others of the scouts. Lenny pulled up, panting, then bent double in exhaustion, gasping for breath. The scouts surrounded him.

'We've been looking for you.'

As yet, Lenny was unable to speak.

'We're glad you're still alive. Did you crash in the mountains?'

Lenny nodded.

'How did you live?'

'Doesn't matter,' Lenny panted. 'Where is Vi?'

'Vi is safe. Come.'

Supporting him between them, they flew back towards the city. Lenny could see that great damage had been done. Many homes and public buildings had been reduced to piles of shining splinters, but many still remained. If Parabolus had meant to destroy it all, he had failed; but if he only meant to warn the Beings that worse would follow, he had made that point.

In the great hall, Oompallah, Asmara, and Vi were all that remained of the great parliament. The other Beings had been sent on missions of

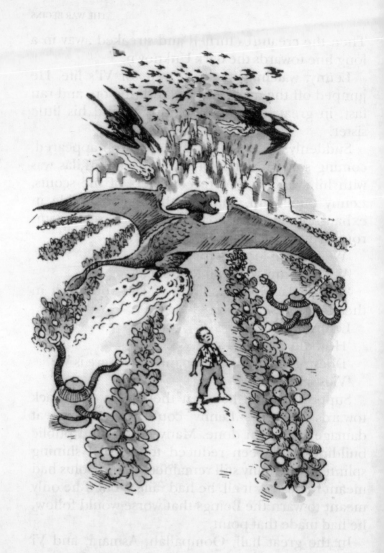

rescue in the shattered homes, or to search for weapons, weapons which they had never used, and didn't know how to use.

'It's a forlorn hope,' Asmara was saying to her daughter. 'They don't know how to fight, or what to fight with. Parabolus will kill us all, even his own mother. Who said we should defy him?'

'Me,' Vi said, 'I said so.'

'Then we put the little human back in her dungeon, and surrender,' the old Being said.

Vi was indignant. 'First you want to put me in prison because I'm supposed to be working for Parabolus. Now you want to put me back in prison because I want to fight him. Please, Princess, don't listen to your mother, she has water on the brain.'

'Don't be rude, child.'

'Well, she's wrong. Please let me be free and help you in your war. Parabolus is definitely the baddy, and I want to help.'

Oompallah came as close to smiling as a Being can, and said, 'Okay, Vi, you can help. Your job in the war is to look after my mother, and keep her safe at home.'

'I can look after myself,' Asmara said, tetchily.

'All right then,' Vi said diplomatically, 'look after yourself, and look after me as well. Why don't we just look after each other, eh?'

Asmara sniffed and spluttered, and grudgingly agreed.

'Okay,' Vi said, 'number one is to find a nice hiding place, safe from the next bombardment.'

Just then, Lenny and Daroo appeared, coming through a star-shaped hole in the roof, and settled beside them.

Lenny and Vi hugged each other. Tears began to stream down their faces, but then, remembering how brave they were, they stopped crying and began to laugh.

'Okay, sis?'

'Okay, brer.'

'Right!'

'Right!'

'You and me forever,' and they hugged again.

The Beings had tactfully withdrawn to let the humans go through this rigmarole. Such display of emotion was completely against the Rules.

'So where was you when I was in prison, man?'

'I can't tell you that now. It seems we have a war.'

'Yes. My job is to look after Grandma Being.'

'Okay, good. I better join the army.'

'They don't have an army, that's the problem.'

'Well, next best thing.'

Lenny turned to Daroo, who was in deep consultation with Queen Oompallah.

'Excuse me, what are we going to do?'

'Think. We don't know what to do, so we're going to have a think.'

'Can Vi help us? She's good at that.'

Vi was called to join in the discussion.

* * *

Oompallah sat on her throne, leaning back with

her eyes closed to show she was concentrating. Asmara, in her flying chair, whizzed up and down the hall, drumming her three fingers on the armrests, and staring at the walls as if the answer to their problems might be written there. Vi, hands clasped behind her back, paced up and down saying 'if' and 'but' and 'maybe'. Lenny sat on the footstool, head in his hands, elbows on his knees. The thinking was so thick you could cut it with a knife.

Finally, Vi stopped before the throne.

'What's the problem?' she asked.

'The problem, stupid, is,' Lenny replied, 'that there are flying creatures destroying the city.'

'Ah, what is the answer?'

'Is this what you call thinking?' Oompallah said, impatiently.

'Okay,' Vi said, 'what do we want to happen?'

'We want them to stop, stupid,' Lenny said.

'Ah. We're getting along fine now,' Vi said, and walked up and down some more.

Outside, the sound of another bombardment had begun. Vi looked out of the window to see the terrible sight, winged dinosaurs flying over the city dropping fire.

'My poor city,' Oompallah said, 'how do we get them to stop? Think of a way.'

'Surrender,' Asmara said, flying by.

'That would work,' Vi said, 'but . . .'

'No,' Oompallah said, 'think of another way.'

'Ask Parabolus to tell them to stop.'

83

'He wouldn't.'

'Shoot them down,' Lenny said.

'We don't have any guns. They're against the Rules.'

'So we're right back where we started,' Lenny said.

'No,' said Vi, 'we know what we can't do,' and she walked up and down again, finally coming to a stop in front of Lenny.

'Tell me more about these creatures,' she said. 'We have to consider their characteristics if we want to affect their behaviour.'

Oompallah opened her eyes, amazed at this flow of words from one so young.

'Them ugly, big, heavy, and they carry burning rocks,' Lenny was saying.

'Can we build a wall so high they can't fly over it?'

'That would take too long.'

'Can we hide the city in a blanket of smoke?'

'There's nothing to burn.'

'We must make them crash,' Oompallah said.

'Good thinking!' said Asmara, whizzing by.

'Is how they fly, Lenny?' Vi asked. 'You saw dem coming over the plain.'

'What you mean?'

'Is flap they flap like a pechary, or soar like a john crow?'

'They flap *and* soar,' Lenny said. 'And what's more they keep dropping what they carrying, and swoop down to catch it again just before it hit the ground.'

'Ah,' said Vi, and walked up and down again, saying 'if' and 'but' and 'maybe' and 'suppose'.

She watched Asmara and the flying chair making circles round the throne.

'How does she fly?'

'Everybody knows that,' Lenny said. 'There's an anti-gravity engine in the bottom of her chair.'

'So, if you switch it off?'

'She would crash.'

'Suppose ...' Vi said, 'just suppose ... that's the answer!' she said, and jumped up and down. 'That's the answer if ...'

'If what?'

'Can we stop them flying?' Oompallah said.

'No problem,' Vi replied.

* * *

Following Vi's instructions, Lenny, Daroo and the scouts left the city early in the morning and went into the fields. They fanned out in an irregular line, making a sort of zone of defence between the city and the Unknown. Each of them had brought his pogo-stick but had not used it, to save power. Instead, they half-buried the pogo-sticks, handle in the ground and base pointing upwards. When they had done that, and tested them for firmness, the scouts withdrew, armed only with remote controls, and waited for the attacking dinosaurs.

They came, a dark cloud of winged monsters bearing fire, bobbing up and down. When the first flew overhead, and dropped his burning load, Lonny switched on his anti-gravity, *putting it in reverse*. The falling rock suddenly doubled in weight, and the dinosaur, swooping to catch it, missed, overbalanced like a diving pelican, crashed, and broke its neck. All up and down the plain this was repeated, and the fields were buried in a rain of fire, and crashing dinosaurs lay dying everywhere.

Vi, watching from the tower of the great hall, turned to Oompallah, 'There we are,' she said, 'no problem.'

General Vi

Next day, the bodies of the dinosaurs were gone. The wind no longer fluttered through their broken wings. The fields that had been littered with scaly legs, thick tails, and staring eyes were once more clean and orderly. The slave machines were back at work, picking fruit and planting greens for the markets of the city.

'Where you t'ink them gone?' Vi asked Lenny.

'Search me. Things does have a way of disappearing on this planet.'

'We never imagine them,' Vi said, looking down from the tower at the devastation of the city.

'No way. I have a notion,' Lenny said, searching for one of his phrases, 'they were a manifestation.'

'A manifestation of what?'

'The energy of evil,' Lenny said.

'Oh, okay, right,' Vi said chirpily, 'you not so dumb as you look. You saying that Parabolus has withdrawn his energy, so he planning to use it in another form.'

'Something worse.'

'What could be worse?'

Looking the other way, they saw that the repairs to the city had begun. As everything was built out of a glassy substance the shattering and splintering

had been serious. The streets looked like a dump
for broken bottles. Patching things with a little
mortar or cement was quite impossible, and
because the planet had been so long at peace and
buildings only fell down every once in a while there
was a shortage of construction machines. So the
machines that constructed construction machines
had to dust themselves off, and go to work double
quick. The construction machines, in their turn,
had to scoop up broken buildings and load them
into trucks. The trucks took them to be melted
down, poured and rolled, shaped and cooled,
made into sections, and sent back as pre-fabricated
portions of a brand-new house.

Meanwhile, the Beings moaned and groaned
and wrapped their wounds in bandages. There was
nothing else to do. The machines knew all the
jobs, and they knew nothing. So the Beings had to
wait for the city to be rebuilt before they could
resume their lives, eating and sleeping, exercising,
talking, making friends, singing their complicated
songs, dancing their stately dances, and thinking
lofty thoughts.

It hadn't got to that stage yet when the ever-
watchful Daroo spotted the next attack. He
thought at first that the dark limit of the Unknown
was closer than usual. The next day it was closer
still. Something was moving so slowly over the
plain that its movement was hardly visible. With
Lenny and Lilas, he organized a reconnaissance
flight, and they whizzed over to have a look.

It was a line, a herd, a sea of giant tortoises, advancing relentlessly, step by slow step across the plain. They were armour plated, each shell the size of a cathedral dome, legs like the trunks of cotton trees, and heads like whole elephants, a lot of heads. Lenny thought they must be looking over each other's shoulders, and continually leaning sideways to consult their neighbours.

The truth, he suddenly realized, was that each of the tortoises had four heads, north, south, east and west. They were able to move forward or backward without ever turning round. However, with four heads and eight eyes all sending messages to the brain at the same time, information had to be carefully sorted and considered before the nervous system could respond. So this multiplicity of legs and extravagance of heads made the progress of the tortoise army ponderously slow.

On they came, plod after plod, a rolling ocean of shells, a forest of heads with beady eyes and snapping mouths.

'They'll walk all over the city, and crush us all to death,' said Lilas fearfully.

'Let's go back,' Daroo said.

'Vi will think of something,' Lenny said.

* * *

'A ditch,' Vi suggested.

'And a wall,' Lenny added.

'Like a castle wall, with a moat,' Vi continued. 'The Beings peaceful for so long them don' know

89

how to fight war. So, Lenny, you and I must be de
generals. Let's go see Oompallah.'

So they scurried through the corridors of Oompallah's palace to the great hall, where Daroo was
explaining to the gathered Beings that another
attack was under way, led by giant tortoises.

Lenny and Vi, now respected, indeed honoured
because of their success against the dinosaurs,
went straight to Oompallah's throne.

'What do the humans suggest?' Oompallah
asked.

'A ditch,' Vi said.

'And a wall,' Lenny added.

'The tortoises can't fly,' Vi went on, 'so they'll
just topple into the ditch, head first, and they
won't be able to get out.'

'But they have heads all round,' Daroo said,
'they can just go into reverse.'

'Then they're going away again,' Lenny said,
proud of his brain power.

'True,' said old Asmara, 'they'll be going away.'

The Beings all sighed with relief, as if it had
happened already.

'We'll build a ditch,' Oompallah decided, and
she went round behind the throne to the small
black box which ruled over all the machines on the
planet.

'Tell the re-programming machines to tell all
the agricultural machines to stop farming and dig
a ditch,' she said.

A little green light winked on the black box.

90

Out in the fields, the red and yellow agricultural machines stopped planting seeds and picking beans, and moved in unison towards the advancing wall of tortoises. Calculating the speed of their advance, the machines left enough time for the completion of the ditch and started digging, not furiously, as machines have no emotion, but efficiently and speedily.

Lenny and Vi watched from the great tower.

'It look like dem playing draughts, or Chinese chequers,' Lenny said.

'Generals always say t'ings like that,' Vi said reprovingly. 'But this is serious, this life or death.'

The ditch was dug, and the machines withdrew, but still the tortoises came on, plod, plod, plod. The first of them toppled into the great ditch, and then the next, all up and down the front rank. They slid, they tilted and they rolled into the yawning trap. The Beings, watching from the city, smiled, and patted each other on the back.

'You win again, Vi,' Lenny said.

The relief was short lived, for the second rank of tortoises just plodded on, filling up the ditch, trampling on each other's shells. They pushed the wall down, and came on, advancing relentlessly towards the city.

'You needs to t'ink of something better, Vi.'

'Why me? It always me. I suppose you going to blame me when we dead. When those things crush us all to death you'll say it's because Vi didn't t'ink of somet'ing.'

91

'Yes,' Lenny said, 'das exactly what I'll say.'

Oompallah called another conference, with Vi and Lenny by the throne. The matter was urgent now, the tortoises were so close you could see their bleary eyes with the city reflected in them, close and plodding ever closer.

The Beings whispered among themselves, 'Try feeding them', 'Try begging them to stop', 'Surrender', and 'Beg Parabolus for mercy'.

Vi paid no attention to all that, letting their words pass over her like the wind. She sat on the footstool staring at the floor, concentrating. The ditch didn't work, she thought, the wall didn't work, we have no weapons. The solution to this problem must be in the tortoises themselves, and you can't talk to them, can't reason with them, because they are so slow-witted. Slow-witted.

'Sssh!' Vi said.

'Sssh!' Lenny repeated. 'She's thinking.'

There was silence in the hall.

'Slow-witted,' Vi said out loud.

You could have heard a pin drop, if there had been a pin to drop.

'Can you ask the black box to ask the construction machines to make a lot of mirrors?'

'Yes, of course,' Oompallah said patiently, 'but why? What good will that do?'

'Not just mirrors,' Vi went on, 'but those silly ones that make you fat or thin, or near or far, or all mixed-up.'

'Please explain,' Oompallah said.

92

So Vi explained what was to be done, by whom, and how, and all the Beings nodded, as they do.

'Dis better work, Vi,' Lenny said.

'Cross fingers.'

* * *

The bravest of the Beings, armed with mirrors as big as shields, went out to meet the tortoises. They were an army of light, confronting a dark foe. But the tortoises came on. The Beings ran among them, risking being crushed, or snapped at, and presented the mirrors to the multitude of heads. The tortoises then saw themselves as huge, as small, as thin as snakes, as gross as slugs, with a million eyes or a million feet. They saw their neighbours crowding close, or far away, breaking formation. Every eye in every head received a different message, and sent it on overloaded nerves to clog their tiny, baffled brains, which burned and collapsed, quite unable to decipher what was going on.

One tortoise stopped. The next came plodding on, and walked on top of him. Another changed direction, confusing the one behind, and soon the wall of death was broken. There were tortoises all over the plain, wandering, lost, pursued by Beings with their mirror shields, tormenting them.

Lenny, the general, saw his chance, and ordered the second wave of the defence. The construction machines repairing the city were sent out in search of tortoises. Each one found, dazzled, alone, and standing stationary, was attacked by the construction machines. These came alongside, got a fork lift under the shell and tipped the tortoises over on their backs, where they rolled helplessly with giant legs in the air, until the plain was covered with stranded tortoises, their movements growing weaker as the day wore on.

The Peacock Snake

Next day, the tortoises were gone.

Lenny and Vi had breakfast on a balcony overlooking the peaceful plain. The Knosian breakfast of grain flakes and chiwongah fruit had never tasted so good.

'So we finish we work,' Lenny said. 'Job done, no problem.'

'Is wishful thinking. Parabolus not finished yet, and we must use the time to do some positive thinking.'

'You think, I'm tired.'

'I think we should go and talk to Oompallah. She his sister, after all, and she knows Parabolus better than anybody.'

So they went through the corridors to Oompallah's private rooms. On the way, they had to stop to let a snake go by as it slithered from room to room. They found the princess up and dressed, re-reading her favourite book, looking for some pearl of wisdom she might have missed the first time. She greeted them warmly, for Lenny and Vi were practically family by now.

'The tortoises are gone,' Lenny said proudly.

'But I was thinking,' Oompallah replied, 'that three is a magic number, and so far we've only had two battles. What will be the next, and when?'

'And I'm thinking,' Vi said, 'that we must understand the first and the second, because otherwise we're going to be baffled by the third.'

'Oh,' Oompallah said, 'but they were different.'

'They were the same, because as soon as we won, the bodies disappeared.'

'Things do that here,' Oompallah said. 'We're quite accustomed to it.'

'That's why you don't think about it. You don't see the things that are under your nose. You want to know what it means to me?'

'You're going to tell me,' Oompallah said, eating a sweet.

'They're not real. The dinosaurs weren't real, and the tortoises weren't real, especially because there are no animals left anyway.'

'Maybe in the mountains,' Oompallah said. 'I've heard stories of animals in the mountains, and of backward Beings who still do their own work.'

Lenny heard that and was silent. He had promised himself never to tell on his friends.

Vi was saying, 'If they're not real, they come from the mind of Parabolus. So what is he going to think of next?'

Oompallah closed the book.

'Snakes,' she said. 'If the ancient writings are correct, he'll think of snakes.'

'I saw one,' Vi said.

'Me too,' said Lenny.

'Where?'

'In the corridor.'

'There are no snakes on Knos.'

Well, that was famous-last-words, because there was panic in the city. Snakes had appeared from everywhere.

Yellow snakes were gliding up and down the streets, green snakes climbed the walls, and green and yellow snakes looked in the windows. In all the crystal rooms in all the crystal city, patterned snakes were coiled, with waving heads, hypnotizing Beings, bobbing and weaving to their own hellish music. Fat snakes spilled out of food cupboards, and small snakes hid in pockets, in drinking mugs, and in eating bowls. Snakes were coiled up on pillows, and writhed and rustled under beds. Public places were so thick with snakes the Beings waded through them as through living slime.

Snakes filled the great hall with their hissing, so the Beings, assembled once again, could hardly hear each other speak and moved from foot to foot as lightning snakes darted underneath. One peacock-coloured snake made entirely of eyes had occupied Oompallah's throne, and the poor princess, with nowhere to sit, stood helplessly, wringing her hands. Asmara, in her flying chair, whizzed round and round the hall, unable to land for fear of coils and fangs.

Above the hissing and the rustling of dry skins the conference of Beings slowly came to order.

'What shall we do? What shall we do? We'll drown in rising snakes.'

Indeed, something had to be done. The tide of snakes was up to their knees.

'Bowls of milk,' Lenny suggested, 'put out bowls of milk.'

Lenny had read somewhere that snakes liked milk, and would go anywhere and do anything to get it.

'There's no milk on Knos, and not enough in all the universe,' Oompallah whispered.

'Silly boy!' Asmara shouted, rocketing by.

'Mongoose!' Vi said, struck by inspiration.

'What, what, what?' chorused the Beings, who had grown to depend on her.

'Mongoose! If the evil mind of Parabolus can summon all these snakes, then we can make a mongoose.'

The very word had made the snakes stop hissing, and in the silence Vi called on all the Beings to help her.

'Concentrate, everybody!' she said. 'See this square of stone? Now, all of you, concentrate on that. Look at it hard, and think hard, think of a mongoose.'

'Them don' know what mongoose look like, Vi,' Lenny protested.

'Never mind,' Vi said impatiently. 'Listen to me, everybody. Just look at the square, and think, think of a little pointed head, with small ears and sharp teeth and two brown eyes ...'

Something like that appeared, but fuzzy, indistinct, without a body.

98

'Right, right,' said Vi. 'Think wickedness, and sly, think of four legs and a bushy tail.'

The Beings concentrated again, and a misshapen creature, rather like a dog, appeared.

'No, no,' said Vi, 'try again. It's not as big as a fox, but bigger than a rat.'

'They don't know those either,' Lenny said.

'Shut up, Lenny!' Vi hissed. 'Try, try again. Concentrate and think "Mongoose".'

Lo and behold, a mongoose was on the stone, looking sly and hunted, cowardly, nasty, and ready to run.

The snakes drew back, leaving him room.

'They'll never run away from something so small,' Oompallah said.

'But he's the first of many,' Vi replied.

The mongoose drew his upper lip back from his sharp teeth, and hopped, and jumped, limbering up for battle.

A snake struck at him, and in a flash the mongoose had jumped sideways so the snake's head smashed on the stone. He jumped back again on to the snake's back, and snapped its backbone with a single bite.

'Mongoose!' Vi cried triumphantly, and another came. And 'Mongoose!' Lenny called, and there was a third. And all the Beings cheered, 'Mongoose, Mongoose,' until the hall was filled with a mongoose army of the mind. The snakes fled, pouring out of the hall and down the stairs like water down falls. The mongoose army followed

them to clear the city.

Lenny and Vi, mongoose generals, followed them, directing their sly troops to chase the enemy, to flush them out of hiding, from under stairs, or in some dark, cool place, along a beam, in a pipe, or curled up in a pot. The shrewd mongoose, the wily hunters, stalked and crept, drove them from street to street until the snakes fled into the open, on to the plain, and darted hurriedly away in undulating Ss.

* * *

One snake was left, the royal purple snake, patterned with peacock's eyes. It had not left the throne, but draped itself over the back and arms, and in the middle of the seat, with coils to spare. Its head lifted, it looked down the hall.

On the departure of the rest, Oompallah turned to see it, watching her, its cold eyes and flickering tongue menacing her. She was a princess, so she was not afraid, and she approached it, but stopped as the snake began to change. The outlines of the head blurred, and dissolved, and formed again into the face of Parabolus, that gaunt, white face, with lank, greasy hair and cold, grey eyes, the face the children had first seen imprisoned in the rock. Parabolus kept his snake's body with its gorgeous peacock markings; only his face showed from the centre of the coils.

'This is my throne,' the snake said. 'This is the throne of Knos, and it is mine.'

101

'You lost it because you wanted it, by war and greed.'

'What is mine is mine!' declared Parabolus.

'You did not care for the Beings, or for Knos, not even for the animals and trees. You yourself destroyed what was yours.'

'What is mine is mine!'

'How? Why?'

'Because I want it!' hissed the snake.

'No.'

'You cannot say no. Look! Out the window! See my servants flying in to take control!'

Through the window, Oompallah saw dark shapes, circling like john crows over the dead body of the city, circling, choosing their landing places. They were the same horrid shapes Lenny had seen in the Unknown, shapes with names like Spite, Vexatiousness, Lazy, and Greed. Each chose a high place, a tower, a roof, a wall, spread out over the city. They folded their wings and cocked their heads, and looked down with cold and greedy eyes.

Oompallah, horrified, came back towards the peacock snake, Parabolus.

'You cannot drive me out again,' he hissed. 'Your little friends will never drive me out!'

'Have mercy,' begged the Princess, 'mercy on us.'

'Mercy, Parabolus, mercy,' Asmara cried, whizzing round and round them in her flying chair.

The Magic Words

Lenny and Vi, in the city square, had also seen the wicked things.

'This is the worst,' Vi said. 'This beats all. What we going do about them?'

'Jus' leave it to me,' Lenny said confidently. 'I know these baddies, I saw them in the great Unknown. I heard them talking to Parabolus. That one name is Lazy, that one Greed, that one Spite, and that one Vexatiousness.'

'There's lots more,' Vi said.

'One at a time,' replied Lenny.

He walked around the square, checking out their perches. He saw that Lazy had found a place where he could cock his claws up on a balcony, and let his wings hang down. Greed was not far away. He had his claws sunk into the body of a Being, his wings spread wide, unfolded, and his eyes, unblinking, rolled, looking for something more. His mouth was bloody.

Lazy was too tired to eat, waiting for Greed to feed him.

'He's not going to feed you, you know,' Lenny called up to Lazy, hoping to start something.

'What do you know about it? Greed is my friend.'

'Friends don't mean anything to him, Lazy, he's only interested in himself.'

'Maybe something will be left over,' Lazy replied, and yawned.

'He's expecting you to feed him,' Lenny said to Greed, who did not answer, chomping all the time.

'Lazy is worthless, and will starve to death,' Spite said.

'And serve him damn well right!' came from Vexatiousness.

'Who are you to talk?' Spite said, 'you quarrel all the time, and never do your share.'

'Shame, shame on you,' Lazy called out, and laughed.

Greed said nothing, chomping all the time.

But the quarrel had started now. 'If you laugh at me,' Vexatiousness thundered, 'I'll bite off your idle head!'

Lazy just yawned.

'Do it,' said Spite, 'teach the brute a lesson.'

Vexatiousness pounced, grabbed Lazy in his claws and toppled him off the balcony. Lazy fell with his wings still folded, and broke his neck on the stones below.

Lenny put his arm around Vi, protecting her, and pulled her into shelter. Around them, the Wicked Things had started fighting, every one for himself.

'If we wait long enough,' Lenny said, 'they'll kill each other off.'

'And everything else as well,' Vi said, 'that's the problem.'

* * *

104

Meanwhile Oompallah, princess of the good, and Parabolus, emperor of the bad, were meeting face to face.

'If we keep on fighting, there'll be nothing left to fight about,' Parabolus said, pretending to be reasonable.

'Right,' agreed Oompallah, 'so stop fighting, and go back where you belong, into the stinking mists of the Unknown.'

'Is that a kind word?' hissed the snake. 'Is that the way a princess talks? Shame on you. We must work for the happiness of all.'

'You just said that everything belongs to you.'

'That's so, but out of the kindness of my heart, I'll let you have a little bit. You can have a tiny palace somewhere out of sight.'

'How dare you!' said Oompallah, as haughtily as she could. She drew herself up to her royal height and looked down her royal muzzle. 'This is my planet now! We got rid of you once before, you and your wicked companions. We'll be rid of you again.'

'You can't kill us. You couldn't kill us then, and you can't kill us now,' Parabolus said softly.

'Kill, kill, kill!' Asmara trumpeted, whirling round the hall. But because she could never make up her mind, she added, 'But not my darling daughter, nor my darling son.'

'Please be quiet, mother, and keep calm. No, Parabolus, I couldn't kill you and your friends. It's against my principles, and against my nature.'

105

'It wasn't against your principles to imprison me in a rock for a trillion years,' he grated, and stared at her out of one cold, grey, slimy eye.

'I wanted you to learn the evil of your ways,' Oompallah said. 'In the meantime, my Beings could walk in the ways of peace and love.'

'It didn't work, because it can't work,' Parabolus said, shifting his coils around the throne. 'What's more, it had nothing to do with your principles. I'll tell you why you didn't kill me. If you kill me, you kill yourself. We're brother and sister. There can't be a sister without a brother. There can't be male without female, beautiful without ugly. There can't be good without evil.'

'One must rule.'

'Yes, I must rule. I am the stronger. I am the evil, the darkness out of which all things are made.'

'Kill, kill, kill!' Asmara screamed, rocketing by. 'But not my darling daughter, nor my darling son.'

'I promise peace,' Parabolus said, 'if you give me back the crystal city and the fruitful plain. I'll give you a little bit of the Unknown.'

'What good is that?'

'There are endless riches there, gold and gems, and a multitude of weird creatures to be killed, or tamed, or eaten. The Unknown is full of wonders.'

Oompallah fell silent, her lids lowered over her luminous eyes as she looked into her own mind. She saw no way of getting rid of Parabolus and, evil though he was, peace was better than war. She could not keep fighting forever against flying dinosaurs and equal quartered tortoises, against crawling snakes and circling vultures. She must make peace.

'What about the barren mountains?' she asked.

'Why do you ask?' said Parabolus. 'There's nothing there.'

'Perhaps so, but we better settle that now, just so we don't quarrel about it later.'

'You can have the barren mountains,' Parabolus said generously, 'but I want one thing more.'

'What's that?'

'Those two children. I want them dead!'

'Lenny and Vi! Dead!'

'Yes.'

'No.'

'Why should you protect them? They interfered. They set me free. They are the cause of all your trouble. They're not even Beings! They don't belong. They must die!'

'Yes, kill, kill, kill!' Asmara said, flying overhead. 'Somebody has to die to make a sacrifice for peace.'

Oompallah was deeply troubled, but, as Princess of the Beings, she had to think of their welfare.

'If I give you Lenny and Vi, is that the end of it, Parabolus? No more war?'

'No more war.'

Lenny and Vi had come back into the hall, and were standing by the door.

'You hear that?' Lenny whispered. 'We must run.'

107

'No.'

'We can't fight.'

'No. Trust me,' said Vi. 'I'll think of something.'

'Think fast.'

Vi cocked her head and looked over at Parabolus coiled around the throne, and Oompallah of the gentle muzzle and curled horns and Asmara in her whirling flight. How to get out of this, she thought.

'How big you think Parabolus is?' she asked Lenny.

'He's different sizes, different times.'

'I know that, stupid. How big is he now, in this shape, as a snake?'

'Twenty-five feet long, give or take.'

'How thick?'

'Very thick.'

'Thicker than you or me?'

'By miles.'

'You sure?'

'Sure I'm sure.'

Oompallah came over to them, her long white gown rustling along the floor. She reached out to touch them, to caress them, with tears in her eyes.

'Lenny,' she said, 'and Vi, I love you both, strangers though you are. You have helped us, and cared for us, and joined with us against evil. Are you willing to make the final sacrifice and die for us? Parabolus wants you as the price of peace.'

'Is that so?' Vi said. 'Well, I wouldn't mind. I mean, I've always wanted to do something worthy with my life.'

'What about you, Lenny?'

'Whatever Vi says,' Lenny replied. 'Whatever Vi says I agree with.' He was not *pro* sacrifice but he trusted Vi and thought it wise to go along with her.

'Yes, we're willing to die,' Vi was saying to Oompallah, 'but can you trust him? I mean, when we're dead and gone will he keep the peace?'

Oompallah couldn't answer that. She didn't trust Parabolus either, but if she admitted it then Lenny and Vi would feel badly about being a sacrifice, and it seemed her only chance of saving her beloved Beings.

'Ask him yourself, Vi,' she said finally.

So Lenny and Vi, holding hands, approached Parabolus.

'Is die we going to die?' Lenny whispered to his sister.

'No way,' Vi said. 'Listen, Lenny, when I run you roll the stone, okay?'

He wanted to say, 'What stone?' or, 'What are you talking about?' but there wasn't time, so he just said 'Okay,' not comprehending.

They had reached Parabolus and stood before the throne. Little of it could be seen, hidden as it was in shifting peacock-coloured coils surrounding the grey-faced head of the wicked one.

'Are you ready to die?' Parabolus asked.

'As ready as anybody,' Lenny said bravely.

'And you, little girl?'

'Later,' Vi said, 'if possible.'

109

'Now!' Parabolus said in his rasping, gravelly voice. 'Now! I shall crush you to death, slowly, until your ribs crack and your eyes pop out of your heads, and your guts come out of your mouths.'

'Okay,' said Vi, 'one death is as good as another. But will you keep your promise to keep the peace?'

Parabolus' tongue flicked around his lips, and his cold grey eyes stared at them, but he remained silent.

'You don't even have to say yes,' Vi said, 'just shut your eyes until I count to three. I'll take that as a promise.'

Parabolus did not blink.

'Well,' Vi said to Lenny, 'eyes closed or not, here we go!'

And saying that she scampered for the dungeon where she had been imprisoned and darted down into the darkness. Like a whirlpool of slime, the great bulk of Parabolus uncoiled and sped off in pursuit, down through the narrow entrance after Vi.

'Roll the stone!' Vi shouted from below, her voice echoing.

Lenny ran to the round stone that had sealed the entrance and pushed it so that it rolled in its groove, closing the cave. He knew he was sealing his sister in with the snake, but he trusted her, and hoped the little genius had a plan, because she always did.

Within the cave, the evil thing thrashed round and round, hissing, searching after Vi. She pressed against the rocky wall and edged towards the crack through which she had escaped before. Reaching it she climbed up, just out of reach of the hideous head of Parabolus striking at her. Scratched and bleeding, she pulled herself out again onto the stone floor.

Oompallah saw her first, and ran to help her to her feet.

'Is the stone rolled?' Vi panted.

'Shut tight,' Lenny shouted. 'He can't get out. We got him! We got him!'

'Oh no,' Vi said, 'he'll simply change his shape into a butterfly or a puff of smoke, and he'll be out again making a nuisance of himself. How long does his magic take to work?'

'Almost no time,' Oompallah said sadly.

'Well,' Lenny said, in a burst of inspiration, 'how did you lock him up the first time? How did you keep him in the rock? Remember, Vi? He only got out because I said the magic words . . .'

'Sssh!' Vi said.

'Yes, there were magic words that kept him in,' Oompallah said, 'a magic spell.'

'What was it? Say it!' Vi said. 'Say it quickly!'

The floor was shaking underneath them as if the stones were breaking with the violence of Parabolus' struggle to get out.

'I don't know the words,' Oompallah said desperately. 'My mother knows. Asmara! The words!'

Asmara swooped to a stop beside the throne, her

chair crash landing in her haste.

'The words, mother! The magic words to seal up the evil beast!'

The ancient Being scratched her head.

'I can't remember.'

'You must remember!'

'Don't rush me.'

The floor moved.

'Remember, mother, remember!'

'I can't,' the old Being muttered sadly.

The floor cracked.

A light shone from Asmara's eyes.

'PARUKI ... PARUKI ... SALAMAY ... !' she chanted, and the floor was still. Parabolus was sealed up again, forever.

'Forever unless somebody says ...' whispered Lenny.

'Sssh!' Vi hissed at him. 'You born ignorant, Lenny. That's one thing you must never ever, never ever say again. You hear me?'

'Yes, Vi. I'll always say half a hundred, half a hundred. How's that?'

Lenny's Big Idea

The second imprisonment of Parabolus gave cause for a public celebration. While the machines were picking up the splinters, melting them down, and replacing broken homes, the Beings did some stately dancing in the square and in the streets. Important Beings assembled in the great hall. Princess Oompallah sat on the throne, and Asmara, her wheelchair at rest, sat beside her. Lenny and Vi, at the foot of the throne, looked out at the assembly, at the soft colours of their clothing, the kind faces, and the forest of curling horns.

The presence of Parabolus, so close under the floor, the feeling that evil was just a step away and could at any moment be let loose, gave greater purpose, greater weight, to the contemplation of the good. The Beings were thankful, sober, and joyous.

They were also generous. Not one of them grudged thanks to the little humans who had saved them and brought them happiness. They forgot that it was those same little humans who had caused the trouble in the first place.

Lenny spotted his friend Daroo and waved at him.

'Good times, Daroo!'
'Good times.'

Oompallah made a gracious speech praising the children for their bravery and quick wit, and saying they were a credit to wherever they came from, which must be a marvellous place. Thinking of Jamaica brought tears to Lenny's eyes.

Asmara went even further than her daughter. In her speech she said she knew she wasn't long for that world and must soon sleep in the dust of the planet. But her spirit would live on, she said, and it would seek out Vi and enter her, so that Vi would be as wonderful as she, Asmara, had been.

Lenny poked Vi in the ribs at this, and Vi kicked him in the ankle to remind him of his manners. She didn't want to carry Asmara's spirit around the place, but if Asmara wanted to give it to her, she could at least say thanks.

'Thank you, Asmara,' she said, 'but we hope you'll live forever.'

At this, the Beings cheered, and Oompallah, the serious one, came close to smiling.

Now it was Lenny's turn to make a speech, and imagining himself to be a great preacher he rose to speak, and didn't know what to say.

No, he couldn't tell them about the Mountain Beings, but he could ... maybe ... he could make a better peace between Parabolus and his sister ... maybe ...

Lenny realized he was still standing at the foot of the throne with all the Beings looking at him politely, waiting for him to say something else.

'Talk among yourselves for a while,' he said. 'I want to consult with Vi.'

So Lenny and Vi went off into a corner while the Beings twittered and chattered and grumbled, and Parabolus in the dungeon howled and boomed.

'I is a dreamer, Vi, and silly, but I has a plan to save this planet. Them can't go on like this, bad against good, Known against Unknown. If we say the magic words ...' and his lips moved like saying 'fifty-fifty' without making a sound, 'if we do that and let Parabolus out again ...'

'No!'

'We'll mek him promise ...'

'He bad. He can't keep a promise.'

'He can't promise to be *good*, but he can agree to *share*. If he agree to that, then I can do something for all of dem. I can go secretly to the mountains and bring back some tiny trees, some baby animals, and some little fish that they can plant, and feed, and rear. They can give up machines and learn to work again. What you think, Vi?'

Lenny was so excited by his idea, and so convinced it would work that Vi just had to agree with him.

'Try anything once,' she said, 'we'll say ...' and her lips formed 'fifty-fifty'.

'No, Vi,' said Lenny, 'we can't say it. Is what was wrong last time. We're tourists, we Jamaicans, and dis planet not ours. They does have to agree, and they have to say it themselves.'

So Lenny and Vi, holding hands, went over to Asmara, who was sliding by the throne in her flying chair.

'Asmara, do you want your son to be free?'

'Of course,' Asmara said, 'but he's a naughty boy.'

'Can you make him promise to be good?'

'No.'

'Can you make him promise to be good enough to *share* with his sister?'

Asmara gave Lenny a dirty look. It was a strange idea, but maybe it was worth trying. She moved the chair over to the dungeon stone, and tapped it with her foot.

'Parabolus!'

There was silence.

'Parabolus!'

'Yes, mother.'

'Parabolus, will you share the kingdom with your sister? Two crowns, two thrones, one night, one day.'

'No,' came the booming voice from the dungeon. 'I won't share with that sniffling Oompallah. No, no, no!'

This made Asmara mad, and she shouted back at him, kicking at the stone.

'You'll do what your mother says, do you hear me? You'll do what I say or you'll stay in that rock for ever! Do you hear me?'

Silence. And after the silence, the voice of Parabolus, all humble and sweet.

116

'Yes, mother, I'll share.'

'Will you share with your brother, Oompallah?'

'Yes,' Oompallah whispered.

So Asmara turned to the watching and the listening Beings, and spoke to them.

'My children have agreed to share the planet, do you agree to that?'

As Beings do, they nodded.

'One more question,' Asmara asked, 'and you must answer loud and clear. How will they share it?'

The Beings shouted all together, 'They'll share it FIFTY-FIFTY . . . !'

There was the loudest bang ever heard on that small planet, and the dungeon rock split open!

* * *

Ka-BOOM!

Home Again

Lenny woke up on Grandma's flat roof, looking at
the Jamaican sky, and white clouds shifting over
Long Mountain and Red Hills. His pyjamas were
soaked with dew. Vi was lying on the mattress next
to him, still asleep, sucking her thumb.

Lenny sat up, and reached for his shoes and
socks, but they were gone.

'Vi,' he said.

'Mmm?' she groaned, and stirred.

'Wake up, Vi. We in Kingston, Jamaica.'

'Where else?' said Vi. She sat up and looked
around. Everything was familiar, the roof-tops, the
treetops, the mountainsides in the morning light,
the barking dogs, the crowing cocks, the motor
horns blowing, the people calling to one another,
and all the cheerful racket of a Jamaican dawn.

'I had a dream,' Lenny said, at least I think it was
one.'

Vi looked at him curiously. 'That's funny – I had
one too. Tell me yours.'

'We went to another planet.'

'Go on,' Vi said encouragingly.

'It have a crystal city.'

Vi nodded, 'And people who looked like people
with antelope heads and goat's horns, or some-

thing so, and who were very good . . .'

'And there was a bad guy named . . .'

'Parabolus!'

'Then it wasn' no dream. Two people can' have the same dream.'

'No, it impossible,' Vi said. 'Come to think of it, that's how you know life itself is real, because the person next to you can see it too.'

'Is this real? Jamaica?'

Vi looked. 'I guess so. But my shoes and socks not here.'

'Maybe Granny took them.'

So they got up, and went down the ladder into the garden, and opened the back door. Granny was there, bending over the stove, boiling water for tea.

'Morning, Granny,' Lenny said.

Granny screamed and spilled the water, and hopped around the kitchen on one foot.

'Aah! Aaah! Aah, Lenny. I'll beat your backside for that! You frighten me.'

'Sorry.'

'Where's Vi?'

'She's here.'

'Oh, Lawd,' Granny said. 'Oh, Lawd! Thank God! Come here you little brutes,' and she grabbed hold of them and hugged, and hugged, and hugged as if hugging could never stop.

'Where have you been? Eh? Where have you been? Do you know how long you've been gone?'

'No, Granny, how long?'

'You're playing a joke on me, the two of you. I'm going to beat your backsides for you.'

And Granny collapsed in tears of joy.

'Granny,' Vi said, very seriously, 'Granny, control yourself. How long have we been gone?'

'Weeks! Months! I thought you were dead, you know. I thought you had been murdered. The police said you'd run away and somebody had kidnapped you, murdered you, and thrown you in the sea.'

'No, Granny,' Lenny said, 'we've been travelling through the universe. We've been to another star.'

'Is that so?' Granny said, and her face got very serious. 'Well, I'm going to shut you in your room until you decide to speak the truth.'

'Granny,' said Vi, 'we're hungry. Do you have any food, any fritters, any breadfruit?'

'Girl child, what's the truth of this now? Tell me what you've been doing.'

Vi smiled her broad and innocent smile. 'If you give us some breakfast, Granny darling. But seriously, nowhere, we didn't go anywhere, did we, Lenny? Just sky larking.'

Questions

1 When the children were flying Lenny didn't think they were moving. Why not? How can you tell when you're moving?

2 'Anybody who would lock up somebody for ten thousand years has to be the bad guy, and the captive must be the good guy.' Do you agree?

3 'To be seriously bad is one thing, but to be seriously good could be worse.' What does this mean? Do you agree with it?

4 The crystal city was shining and clean. Why? What causes dirt and smog in cities?

5 When Lenny was on watch, he was nervous. Are you afraid of the dark, and things that go bump in the night?

6 What does Daroo mean when he says 'Nobody ever wins a war'?

7 A Being can only be born when another Being dies. Why? Would this be a better system for earth?

8 The Being language was written in colours, numbers, and musical notes. Are there other

ways of writing a language, for example, ancient Egyptian? How is Chinese and Arabic written?

9 What's Lilas's reason for taking Lenny on the expedition into the Unknown?

10 Can you do any of the sums Vi did in the dungeon?

11 Machines do all the work in the crystal city. Is this a good thing?

12 The Mountain Being says, 'We love our animals, so we want to eat them.' Does this make sense? Do you think we should all be vegetarian?

13 Among the Mountain Beings, males do one kind of work, females do another. Is this a good idea?

14 Among the Mountain Beings, even the little Beings work. Do you think children should work?

15 Do you like the Being Rules? Can you think of any more they should have?

16 What is the weakness of the Wicked Things?

17 Do you believe in magic words? Can you think of any? How about 'Please' and 'Peace and Love'?